MOONSLEEP
AND OTHER STORIES

LIZ TUCKWELL

'A Dead Mermaid on Eel Pie Island' was first published in *MCSI: Magical Crime Scene Investigations.*

'A Monster Met' was first published in *Short! Sharp! Shocks! No 7.*

'Cinderfeller' was first published in *Stories for the Thoughtful Young.*

'Mason's Story' was first published in *Short! Sharp! Shocks! No 7 (print edition).*

'Mirror in Her Hand' was first published in *Fairytales Punk'd.*

'Moonsleep' was a British Fantasy Society's *Monthly Story Project.*

'Scared of Girls' was first published in *Short! Sharp! Shocks! No 57.*

'Some People Smell Roses' was first published in *Harvey Duckman Presents: Volume 8.*

'The Boom Show' was a British Fantasy Society's *Monthly Story Project.*

'The Mysterious Mr Fox' was first published in *Emerging Horizons (ebook only).*

'The Perfect Ham Sandwich' was first published in *Harvey Duckman Presents: Volume 5.*

'The Raven King' was first published in *Weird! Wonderful! Other Worlds! No 1.*

'Tully and the Ghost' was first published in *Harvey Duckman Presents: Volume 3.*

Published in paperback in 2022 by Sixth Element Publishing
on behalf of Liz Tuckwell.

by Sixth Element Publishing
Arthur Robinson House
13-14 The Green
Billingham TS23 1EU
www.6epublishing.net

ISBN 978-1-914170-25-6

British Library Cataloguing in Publication Data. A catalogue record for this
book is available from the British Library.

Printed in Great Britain.

CONTENTS

MIRROR IN HER HAND

I slow my pace as Chanel No. 5 wafts along the dingy corridor and hear a high heel tap-tap-tapping on the floor. Mrs Jennifer Carr is impatient.

I scratch the stubble on my chin. If I'd thought she'd come to my shabby office instead of telephoning, I would have shaved. I want to think she's dying to see me again, but I'm not that vain or naïve. She's desperate to discover what I'd done with her stepdaughter.

Otis Miller, Private Investigator is scrawled in chipped, white paint on the front door of my office. I push it open. The first room has a bare desk, a chair, and a brown couch where I sleep more often than not. This is where a secretary would be if I could afford one. It only takes me a few steps to cross to the inner room.

The loveliest dame I ever saw is waiting for me inside. She sits in a chair in front of my battered desk, legs crossed to display their shapeliness. Golden waves cascade to her shoulders. Unforgettable blue eyes with long lashes survey me. Dark lipstick outlines her luscious mouth. A pale blue dress with a white scatter of polka dots hugs her curves. Her left shoe stops its tapping. I take off my fedora and toss it at the hat stand. I grin at my success when it stays on the hook. It's been a while since

I managed that. I shrug out of my trench coat and sling it over another hook. As I sit down in the chair opposite Jennifer, she leans forward. Her chair creaks.

'Where have you been?' she asks, almost a whine.

'At an all-night diner. Getting an alibi.'

'And?' She pouts a little.

I smile at her. 'All A-OK.'

She holds out her hand. 'Show me.'

She's still wearing her white cotton gloves, although she's placed her straw hat on the desk. I pull a handkerchief from my jacket pocket and unwrap it before placing it on the desk. Inside is a lock of black hair. Jennifer picks it up and examines it, holding it close to her eyes and smelling it. Does she need glasses?

'It's hers,' I say.

'I know. She always used that lemon shampoo.'

Thoughtful of Audrey.

'Black as night, white as snow, red as blood,' she murmurs.

'What's that?'

'Just a bargain someone else made,' she says, a faraway look in her eyes. She nods and puts it back on the desk. 'Any problems?'

I reach over and pull the bottom drawer open. A whisky bottle nestles inside. I pick it up and hold the bottle up to the light. About three inches of amber liquid left. Well, I'd be able to afford a fresh one now – hell, as many bottles as I want.

'Nah. Easy, like you said. Let's celebrate.'

'She didn't put up a fight?'

I give an incredulous laugh. 'Her? She's only a kid.'

'She's sixteen.'

I ignore that. 'And those midgets weren't a problem either.'

Jennifer raises one delicate arch of an eyebrow. 'Midgets?'

'Yeah, she was shacked up with a bunch of midget musicians at a freak show. They call themselves the Zambini Brothers.'

'So, she's dead?'

I allow myself to sound cranky. 'I said so, didn't I?'

She snaps open her black pocketbook and draws out a gold compact. The morning sunlight hits a diamond in the centre, and I blink away the sudden brilliance. It seems like an odd time to powder her nose, but what do I know?

She clicks it open, then raises it to eye level and says, *'Mirror, mirror, in my hand, who is the fairest in La La Land?'*

I'm gaping at her when I hear a tinny voice reply, *'You are fair, beyond compare. Few can challenge you, it's true, but soon Audrey will outshine you.'*

I drop the bottle. It bangs onto the desk. The amber liquid sloshes about but doesn't leak out, to my relief. The compact clicks shut. When I look up, Jennifer's pointing a tiny pearl-handled pistol at me, the latest Ruger LCP 300. It even has a silencer. Nice.

'What the…'

'The mirror never lies,' she interjects, then milks the

pause. 'Unlike men.' She licks her lips. 'It's too bad, Otis. I had fun with you. We could've had a lot more.'

'Like the chauffeur?' I ask.

Jennifer's face blanks for a moment, then she smiles and says, 'Audrey has been telling tales.' She shakes her head.

'Did you have a lot of fun with him, too?' To my surprise, I spit the words out. The thought of some other man kissing and caressing her is painful.

I grab my Remington.

But she's faster. She shoots me twice, once in the chest and once in the shoulder. Even a bad shot couldn't miss at that range. The shots push me back, but I still manage to fire. Burning white hot pain kicks in, and blackness swallows me.

●

I'd tracked Audrey to a travelling carnival. It was their last night in town, so I was lucky to find her. Candy floss and diesel overwhelmed my nostrils. Delighted screams filled the air. Several robots clanked around serving beverages. I bet the crowds gawping at them didn't realise just how many humans were losing their jobs to the mechanical marvels in factories.

Audrey was collecting tickets outside a canvas tent when I showed up. She was even prettier than the colour photo Jennifer had given me. The act was a troupe of seven midget acrobats called the Zambini Brothers. Although if

I were Papa Zambini, I'd have some questions for Mama Zambini; one of them was an albino, one a redhead, and another was a negro.

A helpful bearded lady told me the way to their caravan. I used my lock-picking skills to break in. The Zambini acrobats had given me pause; small or not, seven bodies would be a lot to contend with. Luckily, I'd brought along my Remington Model 9500. This wonder could shoot nerve gas pellets as well as bullets. I made myself as comfortable as I could on one of the small bunks and waited for them.

It didn't take long when they came back. The pellets came in real handy. Soon, the battered and bruised midgets were all trussed up like tiny turkeys, courtesy of the rope in my pockets. Pays to be prepared. I'd gagged them. Seven little men can make a lot of noise. I didn't want anyone else joining our get-together. Conscious of their glares, I flicked open my pocket knife. I bent over her head, and the sweet-sharp scent of citrus disoriented me for a second. I lifted a handful of her glossy, black hair, exposing her slender neck. She shuddered. I marvelled at the smoothness and whiteness of her skin; it was even paler than her stepmother's. I cut a lock, some of the hairs drifting to the dirt floor. Putting the lock into a handkerchief, I placed it in my jacket pocket. Now I had the evidence I needed to prove I'd carried out my task.

Transparent pearls ran down her porcelain cheeks. Her slender shoulders shook with emotion while she cried. Jennifer'd told me that Audrey was a selfish, spoilt brat who treated everyone like dirt. But could I kill a young woman who'd done nothing to hurt me? My hand trembled a little as I replaced the pocket knife in my coat.

'My stepmother sent you to murder me, didn't she?' she asked, her voice young and breathless.

I shook my head. 'Maybe I'm a tramp looking for some quick cash.'

'Then why cut my hair? You want proof. For *her*.' Her voice was thick with loathing. 'I bet she hasn't told you the *truth* about herself. She was my father's second wife, only married him for his money. She encouraged him to order one of those prototypes from his factory, the new rocket cars, a Carr Dynamo?'

I nodded. I knew those beauties, all chrome and curved fins. Way out of my league.

'Then she said he needed a specialist mechanic for it, so he hired a new chauffeur, Joe. He was young and good looking. She started flirting with him.' Audrey's mouth twisted, and I wondered if there was some rivalry there. 'But never when my father was around. I tried to warn him, but he wouldn't listen. Next thing, my father's dead in a car accident, and she looks like the cat that's got the cream. Joe started acting cocky, and then *he's* gone all of a sudden, disappeared. Nobody knows where he went.'

I paced around the caravan. 'What was his full name?' I asked.

'Joe Mercurelli.'

I was tempted to untie her, but I resisted the impulse. Instead, I gagged her.

'I'll be back real soon. Stay nice and quiet, boys and girls.'

Half an hour later, I returned from the nearest telephone box. My contact down at police headquarters confirmed the murder of a Joe Mercurelli.

'Spill the beans. How did you know his body turned up two days ago?'

'Pure luck, O'Malley. Cause of death?'

'A bullet in the back.'

Looked like Mrs Carr was fond of playing with the hired help. For a while.

I released Audrey. At her insistence, I also untied the midgets. They weren't happy. Only Audrey stopped them from launching themselves at me like human cannonballs. Then we had a nice long talk.

•

When I wake up, I'm lying on the floor, my chair toppled over on me. My sneezes reverberate around the office. Nobody's cleaned the floor in a long time. The pain in my chest and shoulder is mostly gone. I push the chair away and sit up. My shirt has a bloodstain on the front and I know there will be a mass of dried blood on the back. I curse. Now, I've lost the one good white shirt to my name. I pull myself up, steady myself on the edge of the desk. I open the bottle of whisky and take a good slug. And another one. Only then do I look over.

A woman is sprawled on the faded rug. The kickback

from her pistol and my shot has thrown her almost to the door. I've shot her in the chest. Unlike me, she hasn't survived. A small bloodstain on her dress and a pool of blood underneath her. The rug is ruined for sure. Damn, that was a present from my Aunt Bessie. Something else to replace.

Steel grey waves frame her lined face. The blue eyes looking up at me are no longer large and lustrous with long black lashes, but small and deep set with scanty lashes. Her thin lips are drawn back in a snarl. Her wrinkled neck looks like a turkey's. She's a skinny old woman.

My eyes widen and my mouth drops open in horror. I retch, and my throat burns. I stare at her, trying to understand. Is this the true Jennifer Carr?

I take another slug of whisky.

The pistol is lying near her right hand, but the gold compact has fallen open some distance away. I pick it up. Metal and crystal mechanisms show through the cracks in the glass.

I whistle. We had shared our bodies, but not our secrets. If we had, she'd have known to load her gun with silver bullets. I try not to howl at the full moon, and I shave three times a day. Audrey hadn't warned me her stepmother was a witch. Maybe she hadn't known. I'm inclined to give her the benefit of the doubt.

This makes things awkward. The plan was to dump Jennifer's body somewhere public so they would soon find her. That would speed up Audrey being able to claim her whole inheritance. But no one would ever believe this husk was the beautiful widow even if the truth was spelled out in neon.

So, her stepmother needs to disappear without a trace.

Now, the unpleasant task of stripping the corpse. Nothing to link it to Mrs Jennifer Carr. I find myself apologising out loud to Jennifer for the indignity. I hope no one ever finds the body, for her sake as much as mine. Fingering the gold compact with the diamond, I half consider keeping it to pawn. It's an expensive bauble. But it's too risky. I wipe the fingerprints off the gun and plan to toss it into a garbage can in Skid Row. I try to stop myself swigging the rest of whisky before nightfall.

When night finally arrives, I dash down to the street to make sure my car is unlocked. As I suspected; no shovel in the trunk. Then I carry Jennifer down to the first floor, her naked body wrapped up in the rug. Her blue-veined feet peeking out from under the rug are oddly touching. I check that the street is deserted and hurry out to my battered old automobile – no Carr Dynamo for me – I open the trunk and throw her in. A car rumbles by and I tense for a moment. I return for her empty pocketbook.

There's a small hardware store on the edge of town. I use some cash Jennifer gave me to buy a shovel, not a fancy electric model, just the basic one. Anyway, you can't use an electric shovel in the desert. The old proprietor raises his bushy eyebrows but remains silent as he rings up my purchase. I'm not stupid enough to make up some excuse for why I'm buying a shovel at this time of night. Nothing to make me more memorable.

•

A moonlit drive into the Mojave Desert sounds romantic. It isn't, not when you have a corpse in your trunk. I keep my speed steady along the highway, not too fast, not too slow, nothing to attract the cops' attention. This far from the city, the black sky is blazing with stars. To my relief, it's a few days from the full moon. Changing into a wolf is the last thing I need at the moment.

The chill air hits me as I step out of the car. Not that it bothers me, my kind don't feel the cold. I'll be working up a sweat soon digging the grave anyway.

I walk a long way – werewolf strength stands me in good stead – until I reach a cactus towering into the sky, and I start digging. It takes me a while. I don't recommend digging a grave in sand, although it's great for the muscles. The grave may not be deep enough to keep out the coyotes and vultures, but my back aches, and I'm ready to crawl into that new bottle of whisky I'd promised myself.

I tip the rug and its contents into the grave and throw in her empty pocketbook. I open the gold compact and stare at the cracked glass. Will it work for me?

'Mirror, mirror, in my hand, Who's the fairest in La La Land?'

The sound is so faint I have to put it to my ear to hear it.

'You are not the one to ask, I have finished now my task.'

I close it and hesitate; I'd like to keep a memento of Jennifer. But it's too dicey. I shrug my shoulders and toss it in the grave before filling it in.

That's all that Jennifer's scheming and murders got her – an unmarked grave in a desert and a bloodstained rug for a shroud.

She must have thought she had it made, so full of beauty and vitality. Maybe it wasn't just the money that had made me agree to her plan. Hell, after our first night together, I probably would have offered to do it for free. Jennifer was right, we could have had a whole lot of fun. We might have spent the rest of our lives together. So what if she was an evil crone? Nobody's perfect.

The memory of her luscious curves touching my body and her face close to mine, eyes closed in ecstasy, those cherry lips, makes me fling my head back and howl at the white orb above. The sound ripples out across the desert, and in the distance, my cousins the coyotes howl with me.

Why hadn't I chosen her? Maybe it could have turned out differently with me than her other boyfriends. I was wise to her games. We would have been a good match. Life with her would certainly never have been boring.

And now Audrey has to wait five years until she's twenty-one to get her full inheritance. Then two more for her stepmother to be officially declared dead. My payment will be a long time coming.

I stand, looking at the grave. My life could have been so different.

A breeze whispers past my ear as if it has a message for me.

You couldn't trust her. She would have double-crossed you and killed you in the end. You'd have murdered an innocent girl.

I'd forgotten my principles for a while there, all for a beautiful dame. I've done some bad things, but I've killed no one who didn't have it coming.

I square my shoulders, turn away, and walk back to the car.

Audrey can hock a few of those fancy ornaments in that mansion to pay me now. After all, she's got her happy ending. The Zambini Brothers will look after her until she gets her inheritance. I've lost the dame, but money makes up for a lot.

And no dame plays me for a patsy.

TULLY AND THE GHOST

Tully's back was propped against the rough stone wall of the cell, his shaking legs stretched out on the packed earth. His sandaled feet narrowly avoided the head of the prisoner huddled opposite him. Only the murmuring crowd could be heard from the arena. The slaves must be raking sand over the blood and guts after the latest gladiatorial bout. He wasn't sure what time the wild beasts would be paraded in the arena, never having been to the circuses himself but it was after noon so surely it must be soon.

After exhausting all the gods of every pantheon to pray to, Tully was playing The Six Steps To Jupiter game to distract himself from his imminent and agonising death. He counted on his trembling fingers.

'One, a dormouse, two, a cat hunts dormice – cats with their sharp teeth and claws – three, Bast is the cat-headed Jyptian goddess...'

The gate to the cell rattled as it was unlocked. It creaked open as the bald arena overseer came in with four slaves, whose arms were piled high with sheepskins.

'We needed those last night,' said a middle-aged man with a thick mop of greying hair.

The overseer smirked. 'These aren't for your comfort, you're to put them on. See.'

He demonstrated, dragging up an old Verminii woman and placing the sheepskin on her back. He pulled the attached sheep's skull over her head before tying strings around her neck and around her middle to fasten it in place. The old woman blinked her mild blue eyes at the overseer.

'Why?'

'Because someone high up thought it would be a laugh.' The overseer gestured towards the iron gate at the top of the short tunnel that led to the arena.

The sunlight threw crosshatched shadows on the floor. Tully was sure that someone high up meant the Dowager Empress Spectacula or maybe her idiot son, the Emperor Tremulous. The sheepskins would make the prisoners twice as attractive to the beasts and twice as slow at running away.

'I refuse,' said the man who'd commented on the sheepskins. He still thought he was someone important. 'I'd look silly.'

Yes, that was the most important thing. Never mind, being eaten alive by wild beasts.

The overseer knocked the man to the ground with one well-aimed blow and began kicking him in the ribs.

'If I say you put the sheepskins on, you put the sheepskins on. Understand?'

The prisoners backed away as if they truly were frightened sheep.

The overseer growled. 'Why me?' he wanted to know. 'We're going to have to do this the hard way.' He jerked his head at the guards outside the cell.

Tully manoeuvred himself to the back of the crowd. He calculated the sheepskins might run out before they got to him. He was wrong. As the guards approached him, Tully noticed the faint red stains on the animal skin. Frozen, he stared at them in horror. They grabbed him and threw one onto him. The sheep's skull banged against his head. A guard tied the strings around him. His back bent under the weight of the rancid, smelly sheepskin.

'You're in for a treat,' the overseer told them. 'You've got baby dragons and drakons out there today. No common or garden lions and tigers and bears for you.'

What did he expect them to do, cheer? Tully wondered what was worse, to be flamed to death or to be ripped apart? He'd no desire to find out. His blood turned to ice and his whole body shook. His stomach churned, and he farted, a warning sign from his bowels. He was going to die.

Tully wondered which god he had offended. Or was it just plain bad luck? A mysterious plague had swept the imperial palace and most of the slaves had succumbed to it. He'd warned them he was a scribe and a clumsy one at that when pressed into service to wait on the Dowager Empress Spectacula.

It wasn't his fault the annoying pet monkey of Senator Spurius Postumius had run up his back and chittered in his ear just as he offered a dish to the Dowager Empress. Fruit had rained down upon her. She hadn't screamed or shouted. With frigid dignity, she had removed a bunch of grapes perched on her head and brushed away the plums and figs nestling in her lap. Then she had spoken without even raising her voice.

'Take this slave to the amphitheatre and have him thrown to the wild beasts.'

Her burly guards had dragged the howling and protesting Tully away.

'Now...' the overseer began.

It was time. Tully swallowed with difficulty.

'Halt!'

Tully stood on tiptoe and peered over the shoulder of the Brutish prisoner in front of him. A tall imperial guard standing just inside the cell. The guard wrinkled his typically aquiline Reemish nose against the stench of the cell. What was he doing here?

'I'm looking for a slave, goes by the name of Tully,' the guard boomed.

Immediately, all the male prisoners with any wits left began shouting, 'I am Tully!'

Tully glared at them but before he could claim his name, the guard sneered down at them. 'Indeed. Well, this Tully can read and write, and I'll want proof that he can.'

Everyone but Tully and a short, black Hethiopian backed away. Tully pushed his way through to the front.

The guard looked at the two. 'And apparently, this Tully is a native born Reemish.'

The Hethiopian started to step back. As he did, the guard clouted him across the face. The force of the blow sent him flying across the room, knocking other prisoners aside.

'That's for wasting my time.' He withdrew his sword and used the sharp tip to slice through the sheepskin's strings, ignoring the howls of protest from the overseer. The sheepskin fell to the ground with a thud and a clack. 'Come on, Tully.' He turned and strode from the cell.

Tully hurried after him, marvelling at his luck, pitying the poor wretches left behind to a horrible doom and wondering which of the gods he had to thank for his escape. The gods were notoriously touchy if not thanked properly for their intervention and he did not want to have to make an offering to every god in the Reemish pantheon. He needed to save as much as possible for his freedom, the pathetically small pile of gold aureii hidden away behind a stone in the wall of his sleeping room. The thought of those coins lost forever, pained him almost as much as dying.

As soon as he had exited the cell, the waiting imperial guard seized his arm.

'Where are you taking me?' Tully asked him.

'What do you care? It can't be worse than the arena,' came the brusque reply.

•

The imperial guard pulled him along, through the long, dim corridors of the amphitheatre, past the iron gate and out into the hot, bright sunshine of the streets. Tully stumbled.

'What's the matter?' the guard asked.

'I can't see.' Tully blinked painfully against the light. He also hadn't slept the night before, too many moans and tears in the cell. He should have apologised to the other prisoners.

The imperial guard scowled but allowed Tully to rest for a moment. A roar came up from the amphitheatre. The screams began. Tully shuddered.

The streets weren't as crowded as normal because a large part of the Reemish population were inside the arena enjoying the slaughter. Plenty of Reemish citizens, slaves, vendors, foreigners and pack animals with carts, and chariots still thronged the city, however. The centurion pushed and shoved his way along the Via Sacra, then through the Forum, passing the huge statue of Remus, the founder of the city, slayer of his twin brother Romulus. Tully bet the emperor hated the sight of that statue; it must remind him every time of his twin brother Timorous, skulking on the island of Kapri.

They moved onto the grander homes on the Aventine Hill and Tully realised their destination, the imposing imperial palace. The guards on duty nodded to the centurion as they walked through the gateway. The centurion led the way to the quarters of the Dowager Empress. Tully dragged his feet. He wasn't sure whether being thrown to the drakons might have been a better option after all. The centurion shook him like a terrier shaking a rat.

'Come on. Best not to keep her waiting.'

They entered the Dowager Empress' quarters. Serenity reigned within, all polished marble floors and painted frescos. The centurion stopped in an antechamber and spoke to an old man seated at a desk.

'I've brought the slave the Domina wanted.'

The man glanced up from the wax tablet he was inscribing.

'She's expecting you.'

The imperial guard pushed open the cypress door and dragged Tully inside.

Dowager Empress Spectacula was seated at a desk, studying a scroll. A thin, middle-aged man bent over the desk, pointing to something. The centurion threw Tully to the ground in front of the desk.

'Here he is, Domina.'

The Dowager empress arched an eyebrow. 'Couldn't you have washed it first?'

Tully was painfully conscious of how he must appear, dirty and smelly in his stained tunic.

'Sorry, Domina.' The imperial guard marched to the side of the room and stood as if on parade.

Tully prostrated himself on the cool marble floor and didn't dare to look up.

'Stand up, slave.'

Tully stood, eyes downcast. The beautiful mosaic on the floor showed Venus rising from the waves. She had a remarkable resemblance to Spectacula.

'Look at me.'

Tully looked. Seen close-up, she was still a remarkably beautiful woman although her hair was now silver and there were crow's feet around her large, dark, liquid eyes and lines around her wide, expressive mouth.

'What's your name?'

'Tully, Domina.'

Once Catullus Valerius Callidus, he had lost his full Reemish name when his father had sold him as a child to pay his debts.

'You're a very lucky young man. I've changed my mind. What do you say to a chance to avoid the death you so richly deserve?'

'Thank you, Domina,' Tully mumbled.

'Speak up.'

'Thank you, Domina.'

'That's better. I've acquired a property, a tumbledown villa in the outskirts of Reem for a remarkably low price. It's rumoured to be haunted by evil spirits. The last owner was a miser who disappeared. His money vanished with him. I think his hoard of gold is hidden somewhere on the premises and I want you to find it. A couple of my men have tried staying the night, hoping the ghost will lead them to the gold but they've always been frightened away.'

Tully gasped. 'But why I will have any greater success, Domina?'

'I don't suppose you will, but it hardly matters if you die. I wouldn't waste anyone useful on the task.'

'But I'm an excellent scribe,' Tully protested, his eyes wide.

'You've been described to me as 'adequate' at best.' Her cool gaze swept over him. 'Marcius and his men will take you to the villa. They will stand guard outside. Do your best.'

'If I find the gold?'

'You can live and return to your former occupation.'

'And if I don't?'

She smiled. 'There are always more savage beasts with empty stomachs.'

Ten soldiers accompanied the centurion Marcius and Tully on the long walk to the villa. It was sunset by the time they reached it. The villa was in a very bad state of repair, doors half off, large patches of plaster showing through the faded paint.

'Might as well have some supper,' Marcius said and beckoned to the soldiers.

They set up camp in the middle of the deserted villa. Tully gobbled down as much olives, bread, goat's cheese and watered wine as he was allowed. He hadn't eaten for two days. No sense wasting food on the dragons' and drakons' dinner had been the arena's practical approach.

Once he'd eaten, he pulled out the writing materials he'd requested. He made a brief, small sketch of the villa on his wax tablet in the fading light.

Marcius watched him. 'A wax tablet won't keep away the ghost,' he jeered.

Tully ignored him. Marcius got up, stretched, and ordered the soldiers out of the villa. Tully had no hope they would help if the ghost appeared, their job was to stop him escaping.

At least, they had left him a lamp. He rushed around the villa hunting for likely places to hide treasure, although the lamp's light was too feeble to illuminate the corners adequately. But everywhere had been searched before. Tiles had been pulled up and holes dug in various places.

Finally, exhausted, he sank to the ground. On the plus side, he was still alive. On the minus side, if he didn't find the gold it wouldn't be for very long. If he did find the gold, could he bribe Marcius to let him escape? Would there be enough gold? Was there any gold at all?

The sky was now black, and stars twinkled above. Then he heard faraway noises, metallic noises. He listened intently. The noises stopped. He relaxed. Then the noises began again, getting closer and closer. They sounded like chains being dragged along the ground. Moans and groans started. Tully's skin grew clammy, and his heart raced. He told himself that a ghost couldn't be any worse than wild beasts. At least, it was unlikely to try to eat him. He wrote on the wax tablet, 'I am not scared of ghosts.' He wrote it again. If he wrote it enough times, he might believe it. The groans and the rattle of chains was almost unbearable. Tully looked up.

A skull with bits of flesh clinging to it, a long white straggling beard and worms sliding in and out of its eye sockets, emerged through a wall. Tully screamed and backed away. Next the rest of the body with chains on its arm and leg bones appeared. The ghost moved towards Tully who ran around the villa but didn't dare try to escape through any of the doorways. He knew the soldiers waited for him with drawn swords. Finally, the ghost backed him up against a wall in what had been the kitchen. Tully whimpered, closed his eyes and waited for the spectre to do his worst.

'Will you stand still and listen to me?' asked the ghost in an annoyed voice. 'I've been waiting to talk to someone for years.'

Tully opened his eyes. It appeared the ghost wasn't going to kill him. He slumped his shoulders and blew out a breath.

'One moment,' Tully said and wrote on the wax tablet, 'Item: One ghost, an old man with a long beard and chains.'

'Hurry up,' the ghost said. 'I haven't got all night, you know.'

'Isn't that exactly what you've got?' Tully asked.

'Don't be cheeky. I need to show you my final resting place so I can have a decent burial.'

'Fine but before we start, what's your name?'

'My name is Plumbius Abito Aurelius.'

'Nice to meet you, my name's Tully.'

'Never mind your name. Now can I show you where my body is?'

'Okay but aren't you forgetting something?'

'What?'

'How are you going to pay for your funeral?'

The ghost cocked his head on one side and thought about it. 'Won't the state pay?'

Tully laughed in his face. 'What, our Emperor Tremulous? Were you a famous poet or soldier or statesmen?'

'No,' Plumbius admitted, looking troubled.

'Then you've got as much chance as getting laid by a Vestal Virgin.' Tully shook his head. 'If there's no money, the best I could do is shove your bones in the earth and hope for the best.'

'But I'm tired of being a ghost. I need a proper funeral.'

Tully shrugged. 'Not my problem.'

The ghost thought for a moment. Tully pretended not to watch him.

'How much would it cost?'

Tully stroked his chin. 'I suppose you want a decent funeral so you can move on?'

'Of course.'

'Let's see, first there's the procession, you'd want to hire some mimes and musicians and some professional mourners.'

'That sounds expensive. Not too much music and no mimes,' Plumbius said hastily.

'Then just some flute players.' Tully thought the ghost truly was a miser. Only paupers had nothing but a few flute players at their funerals. 'Then there's the cremation. You'd need a nice urn for your ashes. Did you want a eulogy?'

Plumbius shook his head. 'No one remembers me.'

'Fine but you'd still need to pay for a feast for the mourners,' Tully told him.

'Is that really necessary?'

Tully frowned. 'Do you want to move on to the afterlife or don't you?'

'Of course.'

Tully scratched a few figures on his wax tablet and looked up. 'I reckon you could do it for about a hundred aureii.'

Plumbius reeled and clutched his chest, the chains rattling as he did so. 'A hundred aureii!'

'A decent funeral costs money. And prices have gone up since you died. Inflation's terrible nowadays.'

Plumbius sighed and finally said, 'I might have a little money tucked away.'

'Really?' said Tully, feigning surprise.

'That's why I was murdered. Thieves broke into my villa while I was on my own, chained me up and tortured me. Then they walled me up in the cellar and threatened to finish the wall. They wanted to know where my money was, but my heart gave way before I could tell them. They got nothing.' He cackled triumphantly.

'So, they killed you.'

'Yes, but they didn't get my money.'

A fat lot of good it is to you dead, thought Tully although he sympathised with the miser's reluctance to give up his wealth.

'What's it to be?' he asked the ghost.

'Can I think about it?'

Tully wanted to tell the old goat that he was being ridiculous, but he restrained himself. Partly so as not to push him to refuse to reveal its location and partly because he wasn't sure what powers ghosts did have and didn't want to find out.

The silence seemed to last forever but Plumbius finally said reluctantly, 'It's a deal. I show you where my body is and where my gold is, and you make sure I have a proper Reemish funeral. Otherwise, I'll haunt you for the rest of your days.'

It was time to come clean. 'I do have to give some of the gold to the Dowager Empress…' Tully began.

'No, no, no!'

'Be reasonable, Plumbius,' Tully urged. 'She sent me here. If I return empty handed, she'll toss me to the lions quicker than you can say 'Boo!' She won't mind giving some of it up to pay for a proper funeral. She's a very pious woman.' He hoped Plumbius had been dead long enough not to have heard of the Empress Spectacula. 'And,' he continued, 'if I'm thrown to the lions, you'll have to wait for someone else to come along and that might take a few more decades. How long do you want to wait? Think of Elysium, the eternal sunshine, the splendid gardens, the pretty nymphs and the delicious ambrosia.'

Tully felt sure once Plumbius was judged, he would be going to the Asphodel Fields or Tarturus not Elysium, but he wasn't going to tell the ghost that. He didn't know if it was the nymphs or the ambrosia that swung it, but

Plumbius finally agreed to show Tully where his money was.

Tully returned to the imperial palace with five full bags of gold and a skeleton in chains. Marcius marched him to the Dowager Empress.

She smiled when she saw the bags.

'Excellent. You have done well, Marcius, I shall not forget this. I am pleased. Escort the money to the treasury and you may return the slave to the library.'

'Excuse me, Domina,' Tully said, as ingratiatingly as he could.

'What?' She did not sound pleased.

'Deepest apologies from an unworthy slave, Domina but you need to know something important.'

'Which is?'

'The ghost told me where the money was on condition that his body had a proper funeral.'

Marcius laughed. 'Who cares about a ghost? We've dug up the body. That should be enough'

'Shut up, Marcius. The ghost told you that?'

'Yes, and he threatened to haunt you, noble lady, for the rest of your days if he does not receive a proper Reemish funeral.'

'Haunt me?' Spectacula was puzzled rather than angry as if she couldn't imagine anyone having the nerve to haunt her.

'I had to tell him who would get the money, he wouldn't tell me where the money was buried, otherwise,'

Tully pleaded. 'He only told me when he found out it was a great Reemish empress.'

Tully thought a little embroidering and flattery at this point was sure to help his cause.

'How much money is there?' Spectacula asked Marcius.

'Just over three thousand aureii, Domina.'

Spectacula laughed, a beautiful melodious sound. 'I think I can spare a hundred aureii.' She waved a hand at Marcius. 'Take a hundred and get this slave to organise the miser's funeral.'

'As you wish, Domina.' Marcius failed to conceal his scowl.

'I do wish. Do not forget that. I shall be most upset if I find out that this funeral has not occurred. I always make sure that the Reemish proprieties are upheld as befits my position.' She jutted her chin, the very model of a Reemish matriarch. Marcius bowed and Tully realised he had better bow too. Spectacula said, 'Oh and give the slave one aureii too.'

'Thank you, Domina,' Tully said, trying to put the appropriate amount of gratitude into his voice. She and Plumbius would hit it off if they met up in Tarturus.

She looked directly at him. 'You have surprised me, Tully, you have done well. I may use you again for some other little errands.'

He should have known. Once she learned a name and attached it to a face, there was no hope of being forgotten by the Dowager Empress.

Tully trembled but managed to say, 'Thank you,

Domina,' again, still not sure he had the right amount of gratitude in his voice. Being at Spectacula the Serpent's beck and call filled him with dread and foreboding. But that was a problem for another day.

She waved his gratitude away. They moved towards the door.

Spectacula asked abruptly, 'Why are you walking so awkwardly, slave?'

'I tripped over a stone during the night and hurt my bottom,' he told her.

She held his gaze for a moment. 'You must learn not to be so clumsy.'

He bobbed his head in acknowledgement and followed Marcius out.

He was looking forward to getting back to the library and resuming a normal life. More pressingly, he was desperate to get to a privy so he could remove the five gold coins he had stuffed up his anus before he had called out for Marcius and the soldiers.

THE MYSTERIOUS MR FOX

Miss Betsy Heysham saw a fox, tall as a man, leaning on a wooden gate. It was watching Betsy and her two sisters walk through the shadowed fields at sunset, making their way back to the old grey manor house, their home.

'Oh look!' said Miss Betsy, the fifteen-year-old, the youngest and plainest of the three, no long lashes or big eyes for her. 'Isn't that a great fox leaning on the gate?'

Her two elder sisters laughed at their short-sighted sister.

'Betsy, you goose!' chided her clever eldest sister, Miss Heysham. 'That's no fox but a handsome soldier in a red coat. Put your spectacles on.'

Miss Betsy was most puzzled when she looked through the small, round glasses. The young man did have a head of hair the exact colour of a fox and wore a soldier's red coat, but she knew in her bones she had seen a fox.

As the three young ladies drew near, the handsome young man called out to them.

'Excuse me, ladies. Forgive me for addressing you without the formality of an introduction but my accursed horse has thrown me and run off. I am a stranger in these parts. Could you tell me the way to Colonel Fotheringay's home please?'

'Oh, you are staying with him!' said Miss Lucy, the prettiest of the three sisters.

Colonel Fotheringay was practically a recluse in the neighbourhood since his only son had died at the Battle of Waterloo. The young ladies supposed that he must be a friend of William Fotheringay, come to pay his respects.

'Exactly!' the handsome young man exclaimed, bowing to them with a flourish. 'Might I enquire who you might be?'

'We are the three daughters of Squire Heysham,' Miss Heysham said.

'Of Greycotes Manor,' added Miss Lucy.

'Greycotes Manor,' he repeated as if committing the name to memory.

'And you are?' Miss Lucy asked, greatly daring.

'Why, I am Mr Fox Fox,' he replied.

They gave him directions and went on their way, not without a few backward glances by Miss Lucy and Miss Heysham.

'He has a very peculiar name,' Miss Betsy said.

'What's strange about Peter Fox?' asked Miss Heysham.

'Peter? No, he said 'John Fox', I heard him distinctly,' Miss Lucy said.

Miss Betsy, who had definitely heard him say 'Fox Fox', told her sisters so.

'Nonsense!' scolded Miss Heysham. 'I declare that you have foxes on the brain!'

Miss Betsy said nothing more and sulked all the rest of

way home. It seemed to her very possible Mr Fox was not what he seemed.

The following day, Miss Betsy went to see Biddy Leamington who lived in one of the most dilapidated cottages in the village. She officially went there once a week with Miss Heysham and the young curate, Mr Smart, to minister to the poor, amongst whom Biddy was counted. However, Miss Betsy spent very little dispensing any homilies or food from the wicker basket she took with her, packed with nourishing soup and such like. Little did her family know that lying underneath the large black bible that lay so ostentatiously on top, was a small red book in which Miss Betsy carefully copied down Biddy's lotions, potions, and spells. Biddy, or so she had informed Miss Betsy, was a witch.

As soon as Miss Betsy arrived at the cottage, she flung the tiny grimy windows open. Biddy made a feeble protest but Miss Betsy ignored her. Biddy was extremely ancient and rather smelly; the only way to spend any amount of time in Biddy's cottage was to open the windows. They got down to work with Biddy happily reminiscing in her rough hewn, high-backed, wooden chair and Miss Betsy sitting on a low stool, making careful notes in her small cramped handwriting.

Biddy accompanied her to the door when she left, expressing her thanks not for the broth or jars of calves' foot jelly but for the small bottle of brandy that Miss Betsy had filched from her father's dark cellars. As they stood there, Mr Fox happened to walk past with Miss

Lucy, she chatting to him and looking up into his face from under her long lashes. Miss Betsy smiled to herself but Biddy asked in a harsh voice, 'Who be that then?'

'Why, that's Mr Fox, a newcomer to the neighbourhood,' Miss Betsy replied.

'He ain't new,' replied Biddy. 'He's old, old as the hills. You keep well away from him, that's my advice to you and your pretty sisters, keep well away! I'll tell you what he is, he's a…'

At that moment, Mr Fox happened to glance up and look straight at Biddy and Miss Betsy. Biddy shrieked and rushed back into her cottage, slamming the door. Miss Betsy pounded on the door, asking what was wrong but all she could hear were shrieks and curses and 'Keep that *something* away from me.'

'Can I help?' asked Mr Fox from behind Miss Betsy. She jumped. She had not heard him come up the garden path. She turned and blocked the door.

'No, it's just Biddy Leamington being silly,' she told him.

Miss Betsy went home wondering what the word was that she had not been able to make out.

There was a ball that evening. Miss Betsy hated the balls that her sister Lucy loved so much. For one thing, she was not very skilled at dancing and for another thing, it took up precious time that she could have put to much better use. Potion making, or eavesdropping, or spying to name but a few of her favourite pastimes. She also almost never got asked to dance, unlike Miss Lucy. Although she did not mind that half so much, as most of the young gentleman danced as badly as she did and she valued all her ten toes. This ball was more interesting than normal because she could watch all the other young ladies making perfect fools of themselves over Mr Fox. So, it was not just Miss Heysham and Miss Lucy who were affected by him.

Miss Betsy was much surprised when Mr Fox walked up to her and requested the pleasure of her hand for a country-dance. She very much wanted to refuse but because she knew that Mr Fox would take it as an admission of dislike, she did not. She was sure that he had asked her only to annoy her sisters and to amuse himself. He danced with a grace unequalled by most of the other gentlemen, a fact they recognised by glaring at him during the dances. Dancing with Mr Fox was not so unpleasant, except for the rather unsettling sensation that she was not holding a hand but a paw, a furry paw with sharp claws. At the end of the dance, he bowed and looked up at her, smiling before moving away. Her hand smarted. She looked down to see little smears of blood on the palm.

As Miss Betsy looked out of the casement window the following morning, early while the dew was still on the grass, she saw a great fox lope up to the windows on the ground floor. He sat on his haunches and looked directly up at her. His long pink tongue slipped out of his mouth and he licked round his dark stained chops, looking at her all the time with his bright green eyes. Miss Betsy's heart hammered in her chest and she drew back from the window.

Miss Betsy dutifully accompanied Miss Heysham and the curate on the weekly do-gooding visit to the village the following week. She made her way to Biddy's cottage as soon as she could and knocked on the low blue door with its peeling paint but there was no reply. She knew from experience Biddy might well be home and pushed the door open. Inside, Biddy's cottage was in a very sad state of disorder. Biddy's chair and the stool were both knocked over and her clothes and utensils were scattered about. The floor was absolutely covered in chicken feathers, they fluttered into the air as Miss Betsy walked further in. Miss Betsy picked up a few grey and white feathers and a couple of the chicken bones and gazed at them for a few moments before she slipped them into her pocket, just as Miss Heysham asked her what she was doing. Why on earth had Biddy killed a chicken or possibly several chickens in her cottage? Why had she not used her garden? And where was Biddy? Then she noticed a few dark stains on the floor. Miss Betsy felt extremely uneasy and alarmed.

Biddy was never found. And in the weeks that followed, several young women, milkmaids and tavern wenches and the like, from the surrounding villages also disappeared. The sisters were told not to venture out alone. Mr Fox had become a regular visitor to the manor house and a great favourite with Miss Heysham and Miss Lucy. This greatly annoyed their admirers, Mr Smart the curate, and Mr Harbinger, the son of the neighbouring squire.

One day, Mr Fox came unannounced into the parlour where only Miss Betsy was sitting.

'I will tell my sisters that you are here,' she said, jumping up.

'Please do not,' he said, walking towards her, 'for I wish to speak to you alone.'

'Me?' she asked.

'You, Miss Betsy. I have a question to ask you.'

'What?' she said, puzzled and alarmed.

He stood in front of her and gazed down at her with his brilliant green eyes. She was very conscious of his body close to hers.

'Miss Betsy,' he said softly, 'would you do me the honour of coming away with me?'

'Come away with you?' she squeaked.

'Yes. Come away with me. '

'And I would do that because?' she asked.

'To run free and never grow old. To be free of obligations, conventions, responsibilities,' he answered, holding her in his gaze.

For a moment she was transfixed. She could picture herself running wild across the fields and forests, a world full of sharp new smells and sounds opening up to her, the great fox at her side, chasing the scent of rabbits. Then a thought slid into her mind. I wager he says that to all the girls. Another thought slid in and hissed, I wager he said that to all those girls. She stepped back and said to him, 'Thank you, sir, for your offer but I cannot accept.'

'Are you sure?' he asked. 'Be very sure, Miss Betsy.'

'I am sure,' she said.

He bowed. 'So be it. A pity.'

At that moment, Miss Lucy and Miss Heysham came into the parlour and he turned laughing to them. 'I would be most honoured if you would accompany me on a little jaunt to Middlestone Woods tomorrow.'

It was a nearby beauty spot. Miss Heysham and Miss Lucy were all excitement.

'And Miss Betsy as well,' he added with a bow.

Miss Heysham and Miss Lucy were all surprise.

'I think Mama will allow it if you are with us,' Miss Heysham said. 'She would not want us to go abroad without a gentleman to protect us.'

Miss Betsy thought about Middlestone Woods being near no human habitation with no one to call on for help.

Miss Betsy remembered that somewhere in the little red book was a recipe for a potion to turn all things back to their true form. She finally came across it late that night in the bedroom after Mr Fox had departed and after her older sisters yawned their way to bed. It had taken her several long hours and a whole candle to find it.

The next day, the weather was perfect for a picnic. Miss Betsy had hoped for dark grey clouds and heavy rain so that outing might be called off but these clouds were fat white ones, which meandered lazily over a bright blue sky. They settled themselves in a field by Middlestone Woods to partake of a cold collation before continuing on to walk in the woods. In the distance, they could hear the faint baying of the hounds intent on a fox hunt.

Miss Heysham handed Mr Fox a pewter goblet, which contained not only madeira but some drops from a little bottle in Miss Betsy's side pocket. He tossed back the draught in one go.

'Bravo!' exclaimed Miss Lucy and clapped her hands. He bowed gracefully to her. The sound of the hounds grew louder.

'I hope they keep away,' Miss Heysham said.

'Curse all hounds and curse all hunts,' Mr Fox said softly and smiled to take the sting out of his words.

Miss Betsy in the meantime was chanting, almost under her breath, 'Masquerader come, Masquerader go, Masquerader, Masquerader, Your true face show.'

It sounded absurd and Miss Heysham said to her sharply, 'Really Betsy, what are you mumbling? You get dafter every day, you really do.'

At that, Mr Fox turned his head and fixed Miss Betsy with a quizzical stare. Miss Betsy looked steadily back at him but inside felt great despair. The potion she had so carefully made that morning did not seem to be working. And if it did not work, then she and her silly sisters were doomed.

Then a horn wailed and the foxhunt was upon them, all plunging horses and barking dogs. Miss Betsy could see the intense faces of Mr Smart and Mr Harbinger amongst the huntsmen. The young ladies screamed in alarm and then screamed even louder for there appeared to be a great fox with them, trampling the plates and food as he made his escape. All was bedlam as the men on horseback and the pack pursued him. Mr Fox was nowhere to be seen. Miss Betsy was thoughtful as she gazed after the horsemen. Had she really seen Mr Fox with a bushy fox tail protruding from the back of his jacket? Had she seen his clothes melting away before her and his body changing to that of a fox incredibly quickly? (Much to Miss Betsy's disappointment as she had never seen a naked man and would have liked to have some time for anatomical observation). Then from several fields off, the young ladies heard the terrible sound of a fox screaming.

The next morning, Miss Betsy dressed herself in the same dotted calico dress that she had worn the day Biddy disappeared. She was looking in the mirror to check for stains on the hem when she put her hand in the pocket where she had put the feathers and bones she had picked up from Biddy Leamington's cottage. To her horrified amazement there were no grey and white feathers and chicken bones, only a strand of greasy grey hair, and human finger bones.

She looked down at the strand of hair and the bones in her hand. Biddy was gone and who was there to take her place as witch and protector? Miss Betsy knew the answer to that question. There was only one candidate. The face of the girl looking back at her.

A DEAD MERMAID
ON EEL PIE ISLAND

It was quiet in the garden leading down to the river bank, the only noise the flapping of the ducks' wings as they clambered onto land, and a quiet sobbing. And it was beautiful too with the silver ripples on the river and the soft greenery of the rushes and the willow trees alongside. You wouldn't think Eel Pie Island was so close to Twickenham, a busy south west suburb of Greater London.

D.I. Lis Liszt stood next to her colleague, D.C. Jay Sharma, looking down at the crime scene to avoid gazing at the two supernatural beings on the opposite side of the body.

The mermaid's body was sprawled near the river bank. Her top half was that of a voluptuous, woman with dark brown skin. The other was a huge fish, the scales shimmering in a thousand rainbow colours. Her long black hair trailed on the grass. Her lovely face stared sightlessly up at the powder blue summer sky.

'My Lord and Lady, these are the Metropolitan police officers I told you about. They beg leave to introduce themselves,' said a thin white male human, with an average face, nondescript despite the smart suit he wore. An official from the Department of Supernatural and Mystical Affairs, he would have been completely forgettable even without the mesmerising twosome.

'You have leave, Mr York,' one of the supernaturals said in English with a Caribbean accent.

He was a short, elderly black man, with a long beard made of leaves. He was wearing only a loincloth, which revealed both his muscles and huge amounts of body hair. His left leg ended not in a foot but a large hoof.

'Don't look at his hoof,' Lis whispered to Jay, who was staring. 'He doesn't like that.'

He had his arm around the waist of a tall, beautiful ochre-skinned woman with a cloud of black hair. A large green snake twined around her body and rested its head between her breasts. She was crying, almost inaudibly. Lis envied her ability to cry without red rimmed eyes or a snotty nose.

'My Lord and Lady, I'm Detective Inspector Lis Liszt of the Metropolitan Police's Supernatural Crimes Team and this is my colleague, Detective Sergeant Jay Sharma.'

'D.I. Liszt and D.S. Sharma, this is Maman D'Leau and Papa Bois of Trinidad and Tobago,' Mr York said.

'And St Lucia,' Maman D'Leau added.

Careful, Lis thought. Water spirits had strong charisma and glamour and it was easy to fall prey to it. She would have to warn Jay about it.

'My Lord and Lady,' Lis said, glancing at them and then looking away, 'we're here to investigate what happened to this…' She hesitated and finished with, '…lady.'

'My sister,' Maman D'Leau wailed. 'Cruelly slain.'

Papa Bois patted her hand and said, 'It is good that you have come. You must find out which human did this terrible deed so that it can be avenged.'

Mr York, edging nervously away from Maman D'Leau's snake that had started undulating closer to him, said, 'We don't know it was murder, my Lord. It might have been an accident and we definitely don't know if any humans were involved.'

Maman D'Leau snorted. 'Who else could it have been?' she asked. 'What water spirit would want to slay my sister?'

Mr York flinched and looked away.

'Did you discover the body, my Lady?' Lis asked, trying to change the subject.

'One of Ndem's attendants did.'

'Ndem, my Lady?'

Maman pointed at the corpse. 'Ndem, a mami wata like myself but from Nigeria.'

'And then her maid summoned myself and Maman D'Leau,' Papa Bois said.

'Was Ndem in the same position as she is now, my Lady?' Lis asked.

'No, we turned her over, hoping she was still alive,' Papa Bois answered for her.

'And put her comb and mirror by her, as was proper,' Maman D'Leau added.

Lis stifled a groan. Bang went the integrity of the crime scene.

'What time was this?' Jay said.

'Not long after ten o'clock, the time for the morning session to begin. Ndem was missed.'

'Was she alive last night?'

The supernaturals shrugged their shoulders.

'You must ask her maid,' Maman D'Leau said.

'Do you know the name of…' Lis began when Mr York coughed and said, 'We can provide you with a full list of everyone attending the talks or in their entourage, inspector.'

'We can ascertain the time of death from the autopsy,' Lis said.

'What is an autopsy?' Maman D'Leau asked.

Lis explained what an autopsy entailed.

The supernatural shook her head. 'No, no, no! She will not be disrespected in this way.' Ripples appeared in the river, becoming little waves. Her big snake hissed. Mr York edged even further away.

'You cannot take her body away,' Papa Bois said, frowning. 'We will not allow it.'

'Perhaps SOCO might be able to find some evidence at the crime scene,' Lis suggested.

Papa asked, 'Who is SOCO?'

'That's short for Scene of Crime Officer. They examine the area around the body to collect evidence that might help us determine what happened.'

'We will not have strangers coming here disturbing this sacred site and taking away the body of our sister to defile it,' Papa Bois said.

'No,' Maman shouted. Her snake raised its head and

moved towards Lis, hissing even louder this time. The waves grew larger. Water started to spill over the sides of the river bank.

'I apologise,' Lis said quickly. 'I meant no disrespect.'

'Of course, we wouldn't dream of doing anything that you would disapprove of,' Mr York chimed in.

'No SOCO will come here,' Lis promised.

The snake retreated back to Maman D'Leau. Its head slithered up to her cheek where she caressed it. As she calmed down, the waves subsided.

'I need to mourn in private,' she said. 'Come, beloved.'

She and Papa Bois turned and walked away, back into the house.

'This is a complete disaster!' Mr York burst out once they had gone. 'You've no idea of the effort involved in decanting the residents and making Eel Pie Island secure for these talks. And now this! The Under Secretary and the Department of Supernatural and Mystical Affairs will never live it down. And if the press finds out...' He shuddered.

'The police officers on the footbridge will stop any unauthorised persons crossing,' Jay said.

Good job there is only one bridge onto the island, Lis thought. Although that must have been one of the reasons for picking Eel Pie Island. She didn't think this was the moment to point out water supernaturals had their own ways of coming and going that didn't involve crossing bridges.

'If you could let my officers have that list as soon

as possible, I'd be grateful, Mr York. We need to start interviewing as soon as possible.'

'You must ensure you don't upset them in any way. Treat them with the utmost tact and diplomacy. We can't afford an international supernatural incident. It's bad enough the UK has been forced to host these talks, let alone this happening.'

From the expression on Mr York's face, Lis guessed that these talks were the supernatural equivalent of the Eurovision Song Contest, which nobody wanted to host because it was so expensive.

'Don't worry, Mr York, we're members of the Supernatural Crimes Squad,' Lis said. 'I have a degree in Anthropology and a Masters in Myth, Cosmology and the Sacred.'

And hadn't The Great Unveiling, three years past, proved her degrees had not been the total waste of time and expense her family had repeatedly told her they were? Her useless degrees had got her into the Met and the Weird Shit Squad and fast-tracked her promotion. The Met had been crying out for officers who had any knowledge about supernaturals when the weird and the wonderful came out of the woodwork. When humans realised they were sharing their world with so many myths and legends, many of whom were not at all happy with what the humans had been inflicting on their world.

Mr York looked unconvinced. 'Perhaps it would be best if one of our officers accompanied you?'

Lis stamped on that fast. 'Probably best not, as it might

make the supernaturals associate your officials with the investigation, which I doubt you want, sir.'

Mr York hesitated and then said, 'Oh, very well. I'll get you that list.'

As Mr York stalked away, Jay said admiringly to Lis, 'You knew just the thing to stop the department interfering with us.'

It was strange being at a crime scene without seeing the usual SOCO in blue overalls collecting samples and taking photographs. How were they supposed to catch the killer if they couldn't gather or analyse any forensic evidence? Even Sherlock Holmes had based his brilliant deductions on evidence.

The water spirits' servants lurked just outside the house, observing them. What a cheek. Lis regretted she wouldn't be able to sneak any samples and would have to do everything by the book to avoid any complaints.

Near Ndem's left hand was a gold mirror with the handle encrusted with jewels and beside her right was a gold comb ornately engraved. The grass around her was crushed. Mami wata water spirits liked their expensive baubles. Lis presumed they couldn't take them away as evidence.

'Pure gold, I shouldn't wonder,' Jay said knowledgeably. He had several relatives in the jewellery trade and always wore a thick gold chain around his neck and a heavy gold signet ring.

Lis let Jay take the photographs with his iPhone X. He loved his phone so much, she suspected he took it to bed with him.

They pulled on gloves and gently turned the body over. The back of her head had been staved in. Lis made a sketch of the injury to show Summersby, the SOCO who always dealt with their cases. She couldn't see anything that could have caused the injury. There were no rocks or tree stumps nearby.

Jay whistled. 'Not an accident then. And not a robbery gone wrong as her stuff is still here.'

Lis squatted down and picked up one of the hands. Rigor mortis had not set in but she was unsure as to whether that was due to the heat of the summer day or whether mami watas even suffered from rigor mortis. She wished Summersby would hurry up and write the first textbook on supernatural forensic methods he kept wittering on about.

There were no self-defence wounds on her hands or arms.

'Her killer crept up on her and she was struck from behind,' Jay suggested.

'It's possible but you'd have thought a mami wata couldn't be surprised like that. There's a legend about a mami wata noticing an intruder while she's grooming herself. She slips into the water and leaves her possessions behind. If the intruder, usually a man, takes her stuff, she turns up in his dreams and demands her belongings back and that he only sleeps with her from now on. If he refuses, she puts a curse on him.'

'Wow,' Jay said. 'Hell hath no fury like a water spirit scorned.'

'True but the stories suggest a human couldn't creep up on her. Maybe it was a supernatural.'

'Why would a supernatural want to kill her?' Jay asked.

'I've no idea. Why would a human? We need to talk to her servant and the other humans and supernaturals here.'

But Lis privately doubted they'd get much out of the people, whether supernatural or human.

'Run and ask if there's a tape measure in the house,' Lis told Jay.

Jay eventually came back with the tape measure. 'Had to borrow it off the neighbours,' he panted. 'This is so old school.'

Lis measured the dimensions of the wound and made notes.

They searched the house as best they could without being able to disturb anything. You could tell the house belonged to an artist. It was full of paintings with brightly coloured swirls and squiggles, and small ugly sculptures even before you got to the studio. Most of the residents of Eel Pie Island were artists.

A lackey turned up with the requested list. Then they began questioning the people in the house at the top of the garden.

'When did you last see Ndem?' Lis asked Olusola Eze, Ndem's servant, a large boned woman with greying hair.

'Last night, before I went to bed. I got up late this morning. I was worried she wouldn't get ready in time.

I went to find her and there she was out by the river…'
Olusola started sobbing.

'I'm sorry for your loss,' Lis said. 'Did she often go to the river bank?'

'Every morning. She liked to sit by the river, turn into a mermaid and brush her hair. It soothed her before the day's talks.'

'Have you got any idea who might have wanted to hurt her?'

Olusola hesitated and then said, 'There is a man. He used to live in Nigeria. He offended the Lady, so he left. The Lady was still angry he hadn't promised himself to her so she asked us to find him.'

'Did he come here, to the UK?'

'The Lady believed so. We were still looking for him.'

'What was his name?'

'Akabom Okpo.'

And that was the most useful thing they could get out of the humans, who all claimed to be working for either Ndem or Maman D'Leau. Jay made a list of their names to be checked back at the office. The supernaturals had melted out of the house while they were searching the crime scene.

They searched the house, looking for possible murder weapons. Lis hoped they would be allowed to come again once they'd discussed it with Summersby and he'd given them some pointers on what to look for.

Lis asked if they could speak to Maman D'Leau and Papa Bois again.

'What is that old guy?' Jay asked. 'Is he a water spirit too?'

'No, he's a nature spirit. He's called Father of the Forest or Keeper of the Woods in English. He protects forests and he doesn't like hunters much. He's married to Maman D'Leau.'

'So, what's he doing at the talks? I thought they're about the oceans.'

'I don't know. Perhaps he just came to keep Maman D'Leau company?'

•

Maman D'Leau sat on a chair, her posture so erect, she made it into a throne. Papa Bois stood behind the chair, his hands clutching the top.

'Thank you so much for agreeing to speak to us, again, my Lady,' Lis gushed. She thought flattery and grovelling would get them a long way with this pair.

Maman surveyed them coolly.

'You have manners.' Then unexpectedly, she said to Jay, 'I like you. You have changed your shape. I do that sometimes, man, woman, woman, man. I enjoy that.' She smiled as if remembering a pleasant memory. 'What is your name, again?'

Lis wondered why she was even surprised by this display of the water spirit's powers. Jay kept his transgender status on a strictly need to know basis.

Jay stiffened and blinked but repeated his name. His voice didn't betray any emotion.

'You may proceed,' Maman D'Leau said grandly.

'Thank you, again. Just a couple of questions. How did Ndem seem to you during the talks? Was she worried or frightened?'

'These are foolish questions,' Maman D'Leau said with contempt. 'Mami watas are never worried or frightened.'

Lis tried again. 'Was she concerned about anything?'

'She was not concerned enough about our precious seas and rivers,' Papa Bois said, a note of anger in his voice. 'She was more interested in finding some human that had displeased her.' He snorted in disgust.

Maman D'Leau reached up and patted his hand.

'But she is dead now and I am very sad.' Her face transformed into a beautiful mask of sadness.

'Did she argue with anyone at the conference?' Jay asked.

'No, I told you, she wasn't passionate enough about our cause,' Papa Bois replied.

'I'm bored with these questions,' Maman D'Leau said. 'You may go.'

It wasn't a request but a command.

•

Exhausted from a long day of interviewing and searching, they finally got back to their office at New Scotland Yard, which Lis reckoned was the smallest and dingiest one in the place.

Lis typed up a summary and emailed it to Detective

Chief Inspector Taylor. She didn't want to put the case on the system until she'd heard what the bigwigs had said. Then she scanned her drawing of the injury onto the computer and emailed it to Summersby.

Lis gave Akabom Okpo's name to Miserable Mick, the older police officer who refused to leave the office unless it was to go home, and asked him to try and get a current address for him.

She didn't bother with any small talk with Mick. He preferred as little interaction with her and Jay as possible. The day she'd started, he'd explained his position.

'No offence but it isn't worth the time or energy getting to know you as you probably won't last any longer than the last lot.' Mick was renowned for his sunny, optimistic temperament.

Lis got back to her desk and looked at Jay. 'Don't you think it's funny the way the supernaturals kept insisting it had to be a human?'

Jay shrugged. 'They don't want to get blamed for it.'

'And how are we supposed to solve it if we can't analyse any forensic evidence?' Lis grumbled.

'I've had a look at the photos on the computer. There's nothing useful there.'

Cameras couldn't capture the images of supernaturals.

Lis' shoulders drooped. 'And we didn't get much out of the people at the house.'

'We've got one lead,' Jay pointed out.

•

The next afternoon Miserable Mick ambled over to her desk.

'That feller you were after, he's changed his name, and if that's not suspicious, I don't know what is. He's Adebowale Okafor now. Here's his address.' He handed Lis a grubby slip of paper.

Lis and Jay went to pay him a call in Harlesden, a not so up and coming area in north west London.

His address was in a street lined with small, terraced houses. A tall, good-looking man in his forties answered the door.

'Akabom Okpo?' Lis asked as she showed him her warrant card.

His eyes widened. 'No. My name's Adebowale Okafor.'

He tried to shut the door, but Jay put his foot in the way.

'Come on, Mr Okpo, we know that's your name. Can we have a chat?'

'Why? I've done nothing wrong. I'm here legally, I changed my name legally,' he said. 'Look, I'll show you my papers.' He turned to go back inside his house.

'Relax, Mr Okpo, we're not from Immigration. We just want to ask you a few questions.'

'About what?'

'Ndem.'

His eyes widened and he hurriedly said, 'Come into the house.'

He ushered them into a small but very neat sitting room. He'd started sweating and wiped his forehead with a clean, white handkerchief.

'Why're you asking me about Ndem?'

'Have you seen her recently?'

'I haven't seen her for twenty years.' A thought struck him. 'Is she here? In England?' He looked panic stricken. He tensed, poised for flight.

'Calm down, Mr Okpo. I'm afraid Ndem is dead.'

Mr Okpo stumbled over to a leather sofa and sat down with a thump.

'That's impossible.'

'We've seen the body.'

'Oh my God. I'm safe. I'm free at last.' A tear leaked from one eye. 'Why are you here then?'

'Your name was mentioned to us in connection with Ndem.'

'What!' He sprang up. 'Do you think I killed Ndem?'

'Did you?' Jay asked.

'No. Like I said, I haven't seen her for twenty years. I've been hiding from her.'

'Why?' Jay asked but Lis had a pretty good idea before he even spoke.

'I was young and stupid. I came across Ndem one evening by the river. When she swam away, she left her comb and mirror behind. I could see they were valuable, and I took them.' He swallowed. 'Then she came to me in a dream and demanded that I return her belongings. Before I could say yes or no, I was woken up by a noise. I knew I had to run away and try to escape her. I left her belongings behind. I fled Nigeria and I left Africa.'

'And you came here?' Lis asked.

'I thought if I went to a different continent, she might not be able to follow me. I've always kept a low profile and I kept changing addresses. I hoped she'd never find me.' He sighed.

'I think she was looking for you,' Lis said. He did have a good motive, but she asked the obvious question. 'Can you tell me where you've been for the last few days?'

'Either at work or here, at home. I can prove it.'

Lis let him babble on, talking about work colleagues and his wife who would back him up. She had a sinking feeling that once checked out, his alibi would be sound, and he wasn't their killer.

•

Lis stood in front of the desk in the Detective Chief Inspector's office.

'I hate to say it, sir…' she began.

'Then don't,' Detective Chief Inspector Taylor barked.

'I'm sorry, sir, but I think we need to bring in Mr Jones.'

He groaned and buried his head in his hands on the desk.

'You're sure?' was his muffled reply.

'Afraid so. We have no forensic evidence. There's no CCTV footage we can use. Summersby was only able to give us a rough idea of what the murder weapon might be and we haven't found anything suitable. And our one possible murder suspect with a motive has a very good alibi with credible witnesses.'

'Then get on with it,' he said with resignation. 'Just try to make sure I have as little to do with him as possible. Or the Superintendent.'

'I'll make the call.'

Lis went back out and broke the news to Jay. His response was even more negative than the D.C.I.'s.

'Not that fucking Welsh wizard! Not again!'

'We don't have a choice. We need to solve this case fast and we're never going to solve it without his help.' Lis moved over to her desk and dialled the number.

Frederick Jones answered suspiciously quickly.

'Bore da. A beautiful morning to whoever is calling,' he carolled. Whoever said all Welsh people had beautiful voices had never heard Jones.

'Jones, it's D.I. Liszt.'

'Frederick Llewellyn-Jones,' he corrected.

Lis rolled her eyes; she was sure the double-barrelled name was made up.

'Ah, the beauteous Brahms. How are you today, my lovely?'

And she bet his Welsh accent was false, he'd never crossed the River Severn in his life.

She counted to ten. Jones knew perfectly well she hated her nickname of Brahms which she had been christened with, the minute she had arrived at her first station. 'Brahms and Liszt – pissed, cockney rhyming slang, see?' was how it was explained to her when she protested. Who even spoke cockney rhyming slang these days?

'Fine. Listen, we could do with your help on a case we're working on.'

'The water fairies?'

Lis sucked in a breath. 'How do you know about that?' She could taste the smugness in his voice.

'I have my sources.'

'Well, if you want to work on this case, you had better keep that to yourself.'

'Don't get your knickers in a twist, I'll be the soul of discretion.'

'You will if you want to get paid,' Lis said brutally. 'If I see anything in the newspapers or on the internet, there'll be no lovely crisp notes for you to play with. Comprenez?'

Jones always asked for cash.

'Absolutely. Are you coming to pick me up?' The lazy git.

'No, I am not.' She bit the words out. 'You can make your own way to Eel Pie Island. Meet us there as soon as you can.'

'Remember my expenses include travel.'

'Keep the receipts. Oh, and Jones?'

'Yeah?'

'Public transport doesn't mean chauffeur driven limousines or taxis. It means buses, tubes and trains.'

She hung up the phone before he could protest.

•

Jones stretched in the garden at Eel Pie Island and beamed at them. The setting sun glowed orange, apricot clouds scudded across the sky.

'What a lovely place, full of natural energy. I can see why the water fairies and the residents like it here.'

'Just get on with it,' Lis growled.

'Patience, my lovely, patience. I must get all the preparations right.'

Jones took his time getting ready. He slowly placed a large crystal of a different colour, pink, beige, grey and mauve at four corners, covering the area of the garden nearest to the river. He stood in the middle of the square he had created and beckoned the others to come to the edge.

'Now, I need to mediate for half an hour to draw on the positive energy of the earth,' he announced. 'Absolute quiet, please.'

'Absolute bollocks,' Jay muttered.

Jones frowned. 'Quiet please!'

He shut his eyes and raised his hands, level with his shoulders. Lis nudged Jay to shut up.

After a boring half hour, Jones opened his eyes and put his arms down. Lis was rather impressed he could keep his arms up for so long. Then he produced a large piece of expensive-looking cream paper and a fountain pen.

'The name of the victim?' he asked.

'Ndem, a mami wata from Nigeria.'

Jones solemnly inscribed it on the paper. 'And the date of her death?'

Lis gave him the date and that too, was written down.

She whispered to Jay, 'Start videoing if anything happens. Send the video to Miserable Mick straight after.'

Jay obediently flicked open his iPhone's cover.

Jones put the paper down and lit a fat, white candle. Bending down, he picked up the paper again. Standing straight, he thrust the paper into the yellow, flickering flame, and intoned,

'We wish to see Earth's power,
Take us now to Ndem's past,
Right now, at this hour,
Bring us back at last!'

Nothing happened. Lis heaved a sigh of frustration and thought of the nasty emails she would get from the Finance Department.

Then she thought she saw a shadow. Jones stepped to the side, and she could definitely see a shadow, which became a blurry outline and firmed into a transparent, beautiful mermaid, sitting on the edge of the river bank, swishing her tail in the water, combing her hair and looking intently into the mirror that she held in her other hand.

Suddenly, there was someone else, a transparent hairy old man, clad only in a loincloth. He moved like lightning. One second, a yard behind her, the next, right behind. So intent was she on her mirror, she didn't even turn around as he raised his hoof and smashed it down on the back of her head.

She let go of her mirror and comb and toppled into

the water. He leapt in after her and pulled her out onto the river bank. Then he vanished. The mermaid lay there, her chest heaving for a few moments then she stilled. She too vanished.

Jones blew out the candle and removed the lumps of crystal from their resting points.

The murderer was Papa Bois. But why had he killed her? Was he still here, invisible?

Lis called out, 'Papa Bois, good evening. How are you?'

Papa Bois appeared right in front of her. She stifled a gasp.

'Good evening.'

'Did you see that?' she asked.

He nodded his head. 'I didn't realise you white humans had some magic tricks as well,' he said admiringly.

Jones approached and bowed. 'I'm one of the foremost magicians in the United Kingdom, Papa Bois,' he boasted.

'Not now, Jones,' Lis growled. She turned to Papa Bois. 'I want you to know, the news you killed Ndem is being spread far and wide right now.'

'So no one can blame the humans for this?'

She nodded. 'And there's no point killing us because it won't stop the truth being known.'

He sighed. 'A pity. It should have worked so well.'

'Might I ask why you did it?'

He shrugged his shoulders. 'A supernatural had to die so we could blame the humans and inflame the supernatural community to take action against them. All this talk of co-operation is ridiculous. We cannot trust humans. You are our enemies, and your existence pollutes the earth.'

Papa Bois was a dangerous fanatic, Lis realised.

He continued, 'And Ndem annoyed me. She was more interested in finding an old boyfriend than in the preservation of our planet. She offered no support at the talks. She pretended she was coming here to help when all she wanted to do was to find some worthless human.'

Lis fixated on his words. 'Help with what?'

'We're talking seriously to all the other water supernaturals. We need to protect our oceans from you humans as a first step.' He stopped. 'I'm not going to tell you any more.'

Lis was in a dilemma. She couldn't arrest Papa Bois. If she tried, he would simply disappear. Would the authorities even want her to? It would cause a great uproar and derail the talks, which was the last thing they would want.

But he was a murderer. Had Maman D'Leau known? Was she part of it?

Lis was trembling with rage and frustration. But she couldn't express any of what she was feeling. It wouldn't have been professional or safe. The case had been solved but there would be no justice for Ndem. She glanced at Jay. She knew he would back her up whatever she did but she was not so sure about D.C.I. Taylor.

In the end, she said, 'I won't arrest you.' They both knew she couldn't arrest him. 'But it will be known by the relevant authorities both human and supernatural that you killed Ndem, not a human, as you wanted us and the other supernaturals to think.'

'A gambit that didn't work,' Papa Bois said philosophically. 'There are always others.'

Papa Bois might have been thwarted this time in his objective of stopping co-operation between supernaturals and humans, but he was still free to try again. And there was nothing she could do to stop him.

'Just walk away, Lis,' Jay murmured. 'It's all we can do now.'

Lis and Jay left the house and walked across the narrow footbridge away from Eel Pie Island. Her shoulders slumped as she stared into the dark water. This wasn't one of their successes. The Chief Inspector would not be happy. She couldn't forget Papa Bois' last words. Justice had not triumphed, and the world was in danger. She had always hoped, thought, her job made a difference but now she was not sure. Perhaps it was time to leave the Weird Shit Squad.

SOME PEOPLE SMELL ROSES

Some people smell roses when death approaches. For me, it's a stench.

I was sitting at the airport with my boyfriend Jay, waiting to fly to Lanzarote for a week's holiday. I'd known him for about six months, and it was a leap of faith going with him at this point in our relationship. He was tall, dark, very good looking. Jay never passed a shop window without checking his appearance. He believed in equality of the sexes unlike some Asian guys I'd met. He was always happy to let me pay my way.

I suppose I was using this as a test to see whether our relationship had any future. Would we get on okay on holiday? How would he cope with the tedium of waiting for the plane? He was frowning at the noisy, blond toddler playing planes, zooming around near our seats.

I smelled a nauseating odour at the crowded gate where we would be shortly departing. It was so bad I had to rush past the curious staring faces to the Ladies to throw up. I knelt on the floor, gasping, retching and clutched the cold white ceramic toilet bowl. I remembered this stink from before.

I was six or seven. We were visiting my Nana and her friend, Auntie Violet, was there. It was some sort of celebration, maybe a birthday party. I remember balloons and cake. Auntie Violet bent down for a kiss. Her wrinkled, sweet-smelling face got closer to mine and then I smelt the most disgusting odour in the world. It was that bad I heaved, then threw up all over her large black slippers. There was a big commotion, and they carried me off home to cry in my bedroom. Mum shouted I'd have to apologise to Auntie Violet in the morning.

I cried even more the next day as Mum told me with tears in her eyes that Auntie Violet had gone to heaven. They'd found her sprawled in an armchair at the end of the party. She'd looked asleep, but they couldn't wake her up. I never could apologise to her.

That memory triggers another one – playing netball at secondary school. As the girls wove in and out, trying to catch the ball, I started getting whiffs of a horrible smell. I stood by Joanna Pryce, a tall girl with stringy hair, waiting for Susannah Perkins to try to make a shot. The stench overwhelmed me, and I bolted from the netball court.

Miss Evans, the short, strict games mistress, shouted after me. I dashed down the steps to the path leading to the school. Not enough time to get to the loos. I threw up over a yellow rosebush in the flowerbeds outside the classrooms.

'Why didn't you say you weren't feeling well, Hannah?' Miss Evans demanded as she came up behind me.

'I felt alright before,' I said, a sour taste in my mouth.

'You'd better go to the toilets and clean yourself up. The school secretary will call your mother and ask her to pick you up.'

Mum hadn't been happy about having to leave work to come pick me up.

The headmistress announced at next morning's assembly that Joanna Pryce was dead.

As I rinsed my mouth and splashed my face at the basin, I made the connection. I'd smelt the horrible odour from Auntie Violet and Joanna Pryce, and they'd both died. The stench was so very bad because there were so many passengers waiting at the departure gate. They were all going to die, and soon.

The nice airline attendant fetched Jay over to me where I stood outside the Ladies. I couldn't go any nearer to the departure lounge without having to rush back into the toilets.

'What's the matter with you?' he asked, and not sympathetically.

'Please Jay…' I put my hand on his left arm. 'I don't feel well. Please don't fly today. Wait and come with me tomorrow. I've a bad feeling about this flight.'

He shrugged my hand off. 'You don't know if you'll be well enough to fly tomorrow. You're not making me pay for another flight and spoil my holiday. I'm flying today.'

I took a deep breath. 'I think this plane is going to crash.'

'What? Why?'

'I can smell it. They're going to die if they go on the plane. You will too.'

Jay frowned and looked at me with disgust. 'You're crazy, Hannah. What are you on? I'm boarding now.'

'Jay!' I called after him, but he strode off without a backwards glance, away from the sanctuary of the Ladies.

I watched him and his black leather jacket in the queue. How he loved that jacket. He told me over and over again, how he had bought it in Istanbul a few years ago.

'A real bargain, he'd bragged. 'The shopkeeper thought I was just another dumb tourist, but I showed him.'

The flight was called, and people rushed into a queue. As they disappeared through the door, the stench dissipated.

I knew I had to warn the airline, warn the other passengers, but I hesitated. I was scared the staff wouldn't believe me and would think I was a hoaxer. Jay thought I was on drugs, they might too. I'd end up being arrested and put in prison.

Or they'd believe me, but for the wrong reasons. They'd think I was a terrorist with a conscience. Visions of a windowless cell, a bright light beaming into my eyes and harsh voices, tormented me. I might be tortured, they do that to terrorists now, don't they?

The young airline attendant put her hand on my shoulder. 'Do you need to see a doctor?'

I had to tell her now. I opened my mouth. Then I saw myself in a straitjacket, locked up in a padded cell, shouting at the walls, 'I'm not mad! I can smell when people are going to die!'

There was a long pause.

'No, I feel a lot better now,' I said finally. 'I think I'd like to go home now, please.'

I slumped against a seat while they took my case off the plane. I'd missed my chance and knew I wouldn't try again. The waiting area was empty and quiet. The stink had completely gone. The passengers onboard must have been furious with the delay.

The attendant insisted I took one of those trolleys that they use for old people to the taxi rank. The middle aged, black man driving it made sure I went to the front of the queue and got the next available taxi. Their kindness brought tears to my eyes.

I didn't fly out to join Jay the next day. Flight KAZ879 didn't land in Lanzarote. It crashed and everyone on board was killed.

I took a week off work.

My first day back, I sat on the hot, crowded tube, staring at the headline on the Metro newspaper in my hands.

PLANE TRAGEDY CAUSED BY BIRDS.

Investigators have discovered the reason for Flight KAZ879's crash.

I nerved myself to read the article.

'Blah. Blah. Blah. Most unfortunate that the plane was delayed. If it had left on time, it would have missed the flock of swallows that was sucked into the engines,' commented Alex Ramsbottom from the Air Accidents Investigation Branch.

The newspaper fell from my fingers onto the floor. I stared through the other commuters, who were swaying in uncomfortable proximity.

The plane was delayed because of taking my luggage off. But I didn't board the flight because of that awful smell. I smelt death because the plane was going to crash, but did it only crash because of me? But if I hadn't delayed the passengers from boarding, then there wouldn't have been a plane crash. My mind went over it, again and again, like a hamster on a wheel.

I was ill for quite some time after that. There have been many versions of the dream.

Sometimes I run after Jay, grab his arm and beg him to stay. He shakes me off. I fall to my knees and clutch his leg. He walks off, dragging me behind him.

Or I block the entrance to the walkway to the plane. I refuse to let people pass and implore them not to get on. They shout and laugh at me, pushing past.

Sometimes I speak to the clerks, checking the boarding passes. I beg them not to let the passengers on, not to let the children board. The security guards drag me away.

Or Jay's black leather jacket lazily drifts down towards the sea.

Sometimes the blond toddler with his arms outstretched flies through the air, laughing.

Now, I'm getting better. I have fewer dreams. My therapist tells me I have survivor's guilt. She doesn't know the full story, obviously. I can't change what happened and must move on with my life. But one thought torments me. Because if I smell that stench again, what will I do?

MASON'S REVENGE

No lights. No warmth. No noise. Only silence and the black, jagged teeth of the ruins of Thornfield Hall. Moonlight showed the empty holes that had once been windows. Hunger roaring in his belly, he turned away and lurched down the driveway.

Luck was with him. At the road, a man passing by hailed him as he skulked in the dark shadows of the hedges.

'Have you been up to Thornfield Hall? It's nowt but a ruin now. It burnt down about a year ago. They say a madwoman, kept in the attic, set fire to it and then killed herself, leaping off the roof.'

Mason's stomach growled.

'Are you looking for Mr Rochester?' the man continued. 'He lives at Ferndean now, about fifteen miles away. Best you go to an inn and go to see him in the morning. Do you want me to show you the way to the nearest one?'

In his eagerness to be helpful, he stepped so close, Mason had to move back from the shadows. The man gazed in frozen horror on the face half eaten away, the cheekbone showing through the flesh, and recoiled from the rancid stench.

'My God…' he began.

Then Mason was upon him, grabbing him by both

shoulders. The man struggled to get away. Mason tore at his throat with his strong fingers. Blood spurted out, black in the moonlight.

The meal was good. He liked the soft, warm, delicious, oozing contents he found inside when he cracked the skull open and scooped them out with his fingers. Once he had finished, he was himself again. Better than that, he now had George Lancaster's memories at his disposal. He took a handkerchief out of George's pocket and fastidiously wiped the blood away. He gazed at the full moon, its face as pitted and ravaged as his, deciding what to do next.

He had shambled over the moors for what seemed an eternity to reach his destination, his reason dwindling until his meal. George's memory showed him the way to Rochester's residence. Mason calculated that he could not reach there before dawn. Best to wait here until the next evening. He now knew that Thornfield Hall had a reputation for being haunted and locals did not like to go near the place. He had been lucky, very lucky that George had ventured past.

Mason laid the remains of George's body on the ground behind the hall, as distraction for the rats that thronged the ruins. He made sure he positioned himself as high up as he could get. He had never liked rats when he had been alive. Now he was dead, they were too quick to catch for food and a positive menace. He had awoken more than once to find a rat nibbling his toes.

Then he waited with all the patience he could muster,

whimpering occasionally as he thought of his once beautiful Bertha, smashed on the ground.

The next night, when he judged it dark enough, he came out from his hiding place. He would have to weave his way around a couple of villages to avoid them. A solitary human was easily dealt with; they were normally so terror stricken that they made easy prey. But a group of them might be a different matter.

It took him longer than he hoped to find his way to Ferndean. Trees and bushes thickly surrounded it. The lights of the house were dimly perceptible through the dark, interweaving branches. He wondered how to lure his quarry outside. He could hardly knock on the door and ask for admittance. He glanced up at the sky, paling to navy and then mauve. Dawn was approaching and he must take cover to avoid humans.

He huddled amongst the bushes and trees close to the house until the sun was high in the pale blue, cloud-clotted sky, hoping the crackling twigs and leaves under his clumsy feet would not alert anyone to his presence. The smell of the damp earth assailed his nostrils. He needed a plan. Patience had not been one of his virtues alive but now, it must be.

Yet again, luck was with him. The front door creaked open. He saw a middle-aged woman, respectably dressed, with a man old, he thought at first, from his stoop, and infirm, from the way the woman grasped his elbow and guided him along.

The sun shone on the man's face and Mason was astonished

to see he bore a strong resemblance to Rochester. But while this man was tall and well built, he lacked Rochester's keen eye and commanding presence. This Rochester looked sullen and savage, and was missing an eye. Mason saw the stump of his left hand when he momentarily took it out of its resting place in his waistcoat pocket. It was not until he heard the man speak in Rochester's very tones that Mason truly believed that it was he.

The woman guided him to a wooden bench near the house.

'Sit yourself down, master and enjoy the sunshine. I'll be back in a while with a nice hot cup of tea for you. Do you want a rug?'

'I'm blind, not a septuagenarian, Mary,' was his brusque reply.

She went back into the house and shut the door. When he judged it safe enough, he pushed his way out between the branches and trudged over to Rochester.

The moss-encrusted stones, slimed with green, silenced his approach but still Rochester lifted his head, looked about him and sniffed.

'What's that abominable smell?' and then half a minute later, 'Who's there? Introduce yourself. What's your business?'

Mason was standing a foot or so in front of Rochester.

'Rochester.'

'Who's that? Do I know you?'

Mason gave a rumbling laugh. 'You know me, Edward Rochester.'

Rochester tilted his head to one side. 'You sound a little like Richard Mason but it can't be. He's in Jamaica.'

'Wrong. I never returned to Jamaica after I stopped your wedding.'

Rochester snarled. 'And damn your eyes for doing so. What do you want with me now? What's happened to your voice? What is that smell?'

'The smell of decaying flesh is not a pleasant one, is it? I should be dead, Rochester, but I live on in my rotting corpse because of you and Bertha.'

'What do you mean?' Rochester half sprang from his seat.

'This is what you condemned me to when you allowed Bertha to bite me.'

'Allowed Bertha to bite you! I warned you not to go near her but you wouldn't listen, would you?'

'I might have obeyed you if you had told me that your wife was a zombie.'

'Bertha, a soulless husk? Nonsense.'

'I have only ever been bitten by one person and that person was Bertha. Now I am a zombie. I never fully recovered from the wound she gave me and it eventually killed me. Your wife was one of the Living Dead.'

'Impossible. I would have known.'

'Impossible when you hardly went near her from one year to the next? How much time did you spend with her when you did, a few minutes at most? You left her to that woman, Grace Poole, and she made sure you did not discover her death, and lose her well-paid sinecure. If you had taken the slightest interest in Bertha, you would have realised and ended her misery.'

'But the Living Dead are mindless, drooling creatures. How could Bertha have escaped her room and set fire to Thornfield Hall?'

'Zombies are only mindless when not fed on brains. Grace Poole could not have been careful enough that night and Bertha fed on her.'

Rochester had sunk back on the bench and passed his trembling good hand over his knitted brow.

'You deserve your punishment,' Mason told him.

'You tricked me into marriage with your sister when you knew that she was already going mad and you think I deserve punishment? What of you, Mason?'

'I have had my punishment but yours has scarcely begun. You haven't realised yet, have you?'

'What?' Rochester hoarsely demanded.

'If Bertha was a zombie at the time of your proposed marriage then you were a widower, able to marry again. There was no impediment.'

'No!' Rochester bellowed in pain and Mason smiled his satisfaction.

'You're telling me I need not have lost Jane. I don't know if she is alive or dead in a ditch, and all for a woman who was already dead?'

Mason enjoyed the agony evident on Rochester's face. He was tempted to stop at that, to leave him to live out the rest of his life in sorrow. But he could make Rochester suffer even more by just one bite. Mason bent towards the prone figure and as he did so, the back of his head exploded into agony. Turning, he saw a thickset man and the woman he had seen before, attacking him with stout cudgels. Another blow landed on his face, smashing his nose. He bellowed in pain. Blood trickled down his cheeks. Blow after blow. He only had a few minutes to think his revenge had proved his undoing until he could think and feel no more...

CINDERFELLER

There was once a rich merchant called Anna who lived in a fine mansion. She thought her husband beautiful and her little boy, Soren, lovely.

They were kind generous people, so they adopted a little girl orphan to be a sister for him. Jerymene's green eyes were the same shade as the buttons on her coat that she arrived in, so they nicknamed her 'Buttons'. They were all very happy.

But then, alas, tragedy struck. Her husband died in a plague, and Anna and her children were left alone. Anna mourned her dead husband for some time, but well-meaning friends told her she was being selfish and should think of a new father for her little son and daughter.

Anna roused herself from her grief and soon met a poor widower who had recently come to live in their city. His name was Frederick Stone.

'And he has sons of his own,' said Anna, justifying the decision to herself, 'so the marriage will provide extra playmates for my son and daughter.'

While the widower had a beautiful face, his smile never reached his eyes.

They were married, and Frederick and his sons came to live in Anna's large mansion. Flounce, the elder son, was monstrously fat and hairy. Grizzle, the younger, was horribly skinny, his hair so sparse he bore a bald patch despite his young age.

These quirks in appearance didn't matter, but the boys were lazy, cruel and selfish.

The stepfather doted on them both and instantly disliked Soren and Buttons. It was perhaps, because Anna spent money on them, and not just himself and his sons. Or perhaps Soren's large blue eyes and long golden hair annoyed him.

For a time, all was well. However, Anna's new husband had tastes his previous poverty had not allowed, or were perhaps the cause of it. Whatever the reason, Anna found herself pushed to make even more money and went abroad to pursue more profitable business ventures.

Disaster struck.

Frederick received news, rather casually, that she had drowned.

Despite the lack of income, Frederick carried on with his extravagant ways. To economise, he gradually rid the mansion of servants, pocketing their wages for his own use.

Bereft of their mother, Soren and Buttons found solace in talking about her and remembering the good times. Then Frederick sent Buttons back to the orphanage.

Soren cried great tears and clung to her until the orphanage mistress pulled her from his arms.

'Such a fuss about nothing,' their stepfather said.

As the servants left, Soren was given their chores.

Finally, there were no servants left, and he did all the cleaning, cooking, and washing. His lazy stepbrothers lounged about the house all day when they weren't going out to play dice with their friends.

Soren was often besmirched with the ashes he cleaned from the stoves each morning and had no time to clean them off until the end of each long day. His nasty stepbrothers nicknamed him 'Cinderfeller', because of his dirty face and clothes. This nickname stuck, and soon, he was always called that, his real name forgotten.

Cinderfeller was very lonely, and the highlight of his life were the odd visits that Buttons made. She'd been lucky and was chosen to work at the palace. She would visit, bringing cakes and chocolate and gossip. Buttons sang the praises of the princess; how handsome and clever and kind she was. Sadly, these occasions were rare, as they kept Buttons very busy.

Cinderfeller grew up like that, without any time for his own pursuits or friends or recreation. Until one day, the queen announced a grand ball. She invited all the beautiful young gentlemen of the queendom so Princess Charming, the heir to the throne, could choose a bridegroom. She had rejected all the foreign princes selected for her and declared she would marry only her own choice.

A messenger rode to Cinderfeller's house and presented a bundle of envelopes embossed with the royal crest to the cruel stepfather. Frederick and his sons were very excited when they opened the envelopes. Inside were the royal invitations, one for Frederick, one for Flounce, and one for Grizzle.

'We shall go to the ball, my darlings, and the princess will surely choose one of you to marry,' pronounced Frederick.

'Is there one for me?' asked Cinderfeller.

'Don't be ridiculous,' scoffed his cruel stepfather. 'Who would want you at the ball with your dirty face and patched clothes? Be off with you, the chamber pots need cleaning.'

Once Cinderfeller was gone, Frederick retrieved the envelope addressed to Soren Worthing he had hidden in a book and put it into the fire.

Cinderfeller wept once he was back in the kitchen. He would have liked very much to wear a fine suit and go to a ball, but everyone had forgotten him. Buttons interrupted his crying.

'Don't cry, Soren, see, I've brought you an invitation.'

Buttons pulled out a large white card embossed with gold writing. Cinderfeller gasped.

'I sneaked one out from the pile for you and wrote your name on it,' Buttons said. 'I'm the princess's page and helped send out the invitations.'

Cinderfeller hugged her, which Buttons allowed even though she would have to brush her uniform later. Buttons had even brought a second-hand, bright red suit and worn-out shoes for him to wear.

Cinderfeller added sequins he'd filched from his

stepbrothers to the lapels of the jacket and decorated each shoe with a rose.

The afternoon before the ball Cinderfeller waxed Flounce's moustache. He washed and combed out Grizzle's towering, plum-coloured wig that matched his suit and hid his balding pate. He polished the shoes of all three gentlemen. Finally, he helped them into their clothes.

When they had left to meet the rented carriage, for his mother's carriage had been long sold, he scampered upstairs. He changed into his suit and brushed his golden hair. Then he went down the back steps and out the kitchen door. But as Cinderfeller emerged from the alley that ran alongside the house, he was horrified to see his stepfather and stepbrothers still waiting for their coach. They turned and saw him.

As one, they rushed on him. Frederick plucked the invitation out of his hand and tore it in two. Flounce pulled so hard at one sleeve that it tore off and made the jacket unwearable. Grizzle grabbed Cinderfeller's foot, pulled off a shoe, and tossed it out into the street where the arriving coach ran it over.

Laughing and chortling, they all got into the coach, but not without squabbling about who would sit where, and drove off.

Cinderfeller stood in the street, still as a statue, while one tear coursed down his cheek. Then he heard a gentle voice he had never heard before.

'Dear me, what is this? Why are you crying?'

A beautiful gentleman stood there, wearing a powdered wig and a gleaming pink silk dress. A sparkling tiara crowned his luxuriant hair, and he carried a wand.

Cinderfeller bowed. 'If you please, sir, I'm crying because I want to go to the ball but now, I have nothing to wear.' Cinderfeller gazed dismally after the coach in the distance.

'I must apologise, I have been much delayed, but never mind. It's not too late,' the beautiful gentleman said.

'Too late for what?' asked Cinderfeller.

'Why, for you to go to the ball!'

Cinderfeller laughed. 'I don't know who you are but thank you for cheering me up. But I must return to my chores.'

'Don't you know who I am? I'm your Fairy Godfather Dominic, dear child.'

Cinderfeller stared at him. 'Can this be true?'

'Of course, it's true. Now, let's go into the garden. Make haste, for there is much to do.'

Once in the back garden, Dominic surveyed the area and nodded. 'This will do nicely.'

With a wave of his wand, he transformed four scrawny rats into magnificent white horses. Then a plump duck was turned into a plump coach woman, and two green lizards transformed into footwomen. Next, he turned his attention to a large pumpkin, and it became a gleaming golden coach.

'Get in,' Dominic told Cinderfeller. 'We haven't any time to waste.'

'But how can I go, dressed like this?' cried Cinderfeller. He indicated his jacket with only one sleeve and his one shoe.

His fairy godfather clicked his tongue. 'I was forgetting,' he admitted. He waved his wand once more. 'Don't lose the boots,' he said. 'They're specially made to fit only you.'

'Boots?'

Cinderfeller gazed down in astonishment at a suit of dazzling silver covered with pearls. On his feet were ermine boots.

'Too much,' said Dominic. He waved his wand again and only the lapels and cuffs of the jacket were covered in pearls. 'Perhaps in gold?' mused his fairy godfather. He raised his wand again.

Cinderfeller stamped his foot. 'I'll be late for the ball!'

'Oh, very well.' His fairy godfather lowered his wand. 'Now, remember, Soren, you must leave the ball on time, for on the stroke of midnight everything will return to its normal state of being. Oh, and take this.'

He thrust the invitation to the ball, miraculously restored to pristine condition, into Cinderfeller's hands.

Cinderfeller eagerly assured his fairy godfather he would remember the warning, and Cinderfeller went off in the golden coach.

Cinderfeller was one of the last people to arrive at the ball. The large, splendidly uniformed woman at the top of the long flight of stairs leading down to the ballroom, asked what his name was.

'Er... mm nnn name...' stammered Cinderfeller.

Before he could finish the sentence, she read the invitation and bellowed out, 'Prince Ermine.'

Everyone looked up. The princess not only looked up but kept on staring. It was love at first sight. She rushed up to him after he had descended the stairs and asked him to dance. They danced the night away, and the princess only had eyes for him. Cinderfeller was equally entranced by her.

The other young men in the ballroom grumbled. None were louder or more vociferous than Flounce and Grizzle. The queen smiled to see her daughter so enthralled. She wondered which queendom Prince Ermine came from.

Cinderfeller had never been so happy in his life as he whirled around the dance floor with the princess. He happened to look up at the huge, ornate clock and saw to his shock that it was ten to twelve. He recalled his fairy godfather's words. 'You must leave the ball on the stroke of midnight for then everything will return to its normal state of being.'

Cinderfeller pulled himself away from the princess and ran across the ballroom, pushing dancers out of the way. He dashed up the stairs. Cinderfeller knew he wouldn't have time to get back to his home in the coach, so he ran as fast as he could. But as he ran, one of his boots worked loose, and he stumbled. He kicked off the boot and ran on.

Princess Charming stood stock still for a moment, and then ran after the enchanting stranger. By the time the princess reached the courtyard, she found not Prince Ermine, but one furry boot. She clutched this to her heart. Princess Charming declared to her mother, 'Whomsoever this boot fits, I shall marry!'

They issued the proclamation the very next day, and all the young gentlemen of the land were very excited. They assumed the princess would only try the boot on the feet of gentlemen. There was great surprise when Princess Charming made it clear that she would try the boot on the foot of every young man, high or low.

The ugly stepbrothers and the cruel stepfather were all of a tizzy at their mansion.

'This is your chance,' declared the cruel stepfather, 'seize it with both hands.'

'Or feet,' said Grizzle and sniggered. He got cuffed for his wit.

Eventually, the princess and her guards came to the house of Cinderfeller. Buttons was included in her retinue. The cruel stepfather had taken the precaution of locking Cinderfeller in the cellar.

Buttons took the fur boot off the cushion it was resting on and proffered it to Flounce. First, Flounce sat down and tried to put on the boot, but his foot was too big and his calves too wide. Flounce stood up to complain, and Grizzle pushed his brother out of the way. He sat down and did get his foot inside, but it was clear that the boot was far too big for him. It flopped on the end of his leg.

Buttons did her best not to laugh.

Frederick bit his lip with anger and frustration until drops of blood appeared.

'Are these the only young men in the house?' Princess Charming asked.

'Oh yes,' Frederick assured her. 'No one else.'

'He's lying, Your Highness,' Buttons told the princess. 'There's a young boy in the kitchen who does all the work.'

'Her Highness couldn't possibly be interested in that ragamuffin,' said the cruel stepfather.

'Let him be brought,' the princess ordered. Secretly, she agreed with Frederick, but she was a fair woman and always kept her promises.

Buttons and the guards went into the kitchen, and she called out his name. They heard his faint cry and unlocked the door. Cinderfeller emerged from the cellar. They brought him to the drawing room. Princess Charming at once saw how beautiful he was, even under the grime and rags. Was this her Prince Ermine?

'Please try on the boot,' she said.

Cinderfeller blushed and walked over to where Buttons knelt. He slipped out of his worn-out slippers and put his foot into the boot. It fit perfectly.

'No!' howled Frederick and hurled himself across the room to tear off the boot.

The guards pulled him away.

'It's you,' breathed the princess.

Cinderfeller smiled. 'I didn't think you'd find me,' he said.

'This is my bridegroom,' the princess announced.

She turned to the guards. 'Put those creatures in jail for three days for lying to their princess.'

She swept Cinderfeller out of the house as the cruel stepfather and the ugly stepbrothers gaped in amazement. Then they began to wail.

Soren and his princess married and lived happily ever after.

Frederick was given a job as a palace laundry worker, and Flounce and Grizzle jobs as scullery workers. Buttons was promoted to major-domo of the royal household. She kept a strict watch on them to make sure they worked hard all day long and were given the worst jobs to do.

And no one ever called Soren 'Cinderfeller' again.

SCARED OF GIRLS

Was it too late? Martin lumbered past the secondary school, glancing at his old battered watch. 3:30. It was nearly time for school to finish and he shouldn't be out so late.

He should have gone shopping before lunch. He shouldn't have dallied at the supermarket, trying to decide whether to get Heinz baked beans that were on special offer or his usual supermarket own brand. And he'd not allowed enough time for the bus to arrive or the bus journey.

He tried to hurry but his weight and general unfitness told against him, as did the heavy tartan shopper he pulled along. It had been his mother's, and he was embarrassed to use it with its lurid scarlet and green check pattern but it was very handy. He knew the picture he presented: a fat, balding middle-aged man dragging a shopping trolley. He'd never seen any other grown men using them. As if confirming his fears, he thought he heard young feminine giggles behind him. His cheeks burned, and he sped up, despite the panting it produced.

The shopping trolley was heavy: two large packets of Jumbo Oats, two packets of digestive biscuits, tins of baked beans, tinned tomatoes, tinned carrots, a loaf of white sliced bread, a large tub of margarine, and potatoes.

Oats and tinned vegetables were cheap and easy to store for a long time. Ideal for someone who couldn't get out much. He needed to stockpile before the terrible school holidays began.

But his relief was short-lived. Halfway along the road, glancing behind him (his mother had taught him always to be vigilant) he saw in the distance a red-headed girl in the purple uniform of the nearby secondary school. His heart bounced in his chest. He must hurry more. Teenagers could walk fast; she might catch him up. He shuddered at the thought.

However, she didn't catch him up. He maintained the distance between them. Martin breathed a sigh of relief when he turned into the road that led into the street where he lived. He expected that she would turn off at the end of the road, turn right or left but she carried straight on, following him.

He dumped his shopping trolley, opened his front door, paint peeling off it, and tripped over the threshold. He banged against the doorway. His shoulder twinged. He turned around and heaved the shopping trolley up, over and down. Slamming the door, he collapsed against it and wheezed. He was safe.

Once he'd recovered his breath, he got up and made sure the front door was shut. It didn't close properly anymore. He either had to slam it or check the latch was down. When it was windy, he put the chain on. A strong gust of wind could blow it open, as had happened frequently before. Then he unpacked his shopping.

Afterwards, Martin went into the sitting room with his cup of tea, digestive perched on the saucer. He wanted to watch some TV as a reward for his perilous shopping trip. He glanced out of the window and froze. The red-headed girl was sitting on the wall of his front garden, chatting into a mobile phone. His hand shook. Brown liquid slopped over the cup and filled up the saucer before dripping onto the carpet. His biscuit tumbled to the carpet and broke. The tea cup and saucer followed. He dashed out of the room and into the kitchen, anything to get away from the girl.

•

The girl stayed sitting on the wall, chatting into her mobile, for about half an hour. Martin nerved himself to check every ten minutes from his mother's bedroom, hiding behind the curtains and peeping out. What would he do if she didn't leave? At last, she rose, stretched and sauntered away. Martin breathed a long sigh of thankfulness that she had gone.

He went downstairs and looked at the nasty brown stain on the living room carpet. He cleared up the mess, got down heavily onto his knees, and scrubbed away at the carpet. Good job it was a flowery one. That helped to disguise the stain. His mother would have given him hell about it.

As Martin dunked his digestive biscuit in his fresh cup of tea, he assured himself that it was a one-off. It would never happen again. His thoughts turned to his dinner.

He didn't feel much like cooking. Jacket potato and baked beans it would be. They had never eaten meat. Too expensive, his mother had always said.

•

Martin couldn't remember when his fear of nubile teenage girls had begun. But now it ruled his life.

He'd looked up the word up in the big red dictionary his mother had given him. Parthenophobia. A fear of young girls or virgins. It was bad enough that he could now only go out of the house after schools started in the morning and must return before the girls escaped in the afternoon. That reduced the chance of seeing or being close to any teenage girls as much as possible. Martin didn't go out at weekends, too dangerous. He was okay with pre-pubescent girls and had no problem with boys of all ages.

Martin had lived with his mother in the house for most of his life. He didn't know much about the world apart from what he read in the free daily newspaper and the TV. His mother had refused to have a computer or to let him have a mobile phone. He'd been homeschooled from the age of eleven by her after a few years of torment at a primary school. She had been an indifferent teacher but ferocious with the authorities that he'd do better out of school. She'd discouraged him from having any activities that took him out of the house. And had never wanted him to make friends with anybody. She'd particularly told him to stay away from girls.

Her death from a heart attack a couple of years ago had devastated him. She'd been his only company. The house was paid for and Martin had no income apart from what his mother had left him. He'd never had a job. His mother told him there was no need, and he'd been happy with that, most of the time. She'd refused to consider his applying for benefits and he shrank from the ordeal. He eked out his money as best he could.

•

Martin was cutting his toe nails in the sitting room when the voices began to penetrate his consciousness. He didn't pay much attention to them at first. He was absorbed in the task, trying to make sure the yellowed slivers landed on the newspaper spread out on the carpet. His toe nails grew so fast, he needed to cut them every week. And they were so thick, it was hard to squeeze the clippers shut. One of the many things his mother had insisted on was well-groomed nails. He'd had to trim her toe nails in the last few years. A task he didn't miss.

His ears caught a feminine giggle. He glanced out of the sitting room window, alarmed. He couldn't believe his eyes. The redheaded girl was back and worse, she had brought a friend. A dark-skinned girl with short black hair. They both sat on the wall, chatting away.

For a second, he froze then he jerked up, dropped the clippers and stumbled out of the room, his bare feet crunching on his nail clippings as he did so. Why had she returned to sit on his wall? What were they doing there? Sweat trickled down his back and sweat patches bloomed under his arms. His breathing came out short and panicky. He forced himself to take some long breaths to calm down. He climbed the stairs to his bedroom and hid in there until the sky darkened.

When he returned downstairs, the girls had vanished.

He dreamt that night he crouched in a cage with thick metal bars in a large room that stretched into the distance. A door opened and young girls flooded into the room, more and more, heading towards his cage. He screamed and woke up, his heart thudding.

•

The next afternoon after school was even worse. This time three girls sat on the wall. The new one had mousy brown hair. Why him? Why pick on him?

It stayed at three girls for the next few days.

Then on the Friday, Martin heard their voices as he walked from the hallway towards the sitting room. He lumbered upstairs and went to his mother's room and pushed back the curtains at the side. Now there were four. He noticed the new addition had long, very fair hair before he had to rush to the toilet and retch over the toilet bowl.

On the Monday, a fifth girl joined the group, laughing and shouting and pushing each other about. She wore her long brown hair in a ponytail.

By Thursday, six lounged there. Six made so much more noise, created so much litter. Martin picked up all sorts of debris inside his front garden in the mornings: cans of coke, and lemonade, crisp packets, cigarette stubs and cigarette packets. He wore gloves, of course. He found big bottles of cider as well. Teenage girls smoking and drinking alcohol.

What would his mother have said? She disapproved of both. Martin had never tried a cigarette in his whole life. She'd allowed him a sherry and a couple of halves of bitter shandy at Christmas and on his birthday. He'd once daringly bought a bottle of cider as a teenager and tried it in secret but she'd smelt it on his breath and sent him to bed without any supper.

•

High pitched swearing followed him as Martin came down the stairs and he nearly slipped in his hurry to reach the sitting room. One of his grey felt slippers fell off. How could he have been so stupid as to leave the curtains open? He'd thought he had plenty of time to close them.

Martin raced into the room and stopped to face the fireplace. He didn't dare look at the curtains in case he saw the girls. He felt for the white cord. He tugged it and the left-hand curtain closed in jerks.

Now came the worst bit. He needed to run past the window to pull the cord for the right-hand curtain. Martin looked straight ahead but despite himself, his gazed shifted to the outside view. There, on the wall of his front garden, sat six teenage girls, some in jeans, some in short skirts. Martin immediately looked away, but the damage was done. They held their cans up in ironic salute. He yanked frantically at the cord and the right-hand curtain juddered along until it closed.

His heart pounded. He collapsed on the sagging navy blue sofa and closed his eyes. He pulled a check cotton handkerchief out of his trouser pocket and wiped his forehead slick with perspiration. But he couldn't rest there until his body cooled down, because of the girls, their voices increasing in volume, constantly reminding him of their presence.

He went into the kitchen for a drink of water to ease his dry throat. As he drank it, he mulled over his options. He could return to the sitting room and switch on the TV and turn it up to full volume, which hurt his ears or go upstairs to the back bedroom and shut the door. He chose the latter and refilled his glass in the kitchen before lumbering upstairs.

Martin had thought about moving into his mother's bedroom after she died. Hers was the larger bedroom. But she had died in the double bed with the old-fashioned quilt on top. He felt queasy about sleeping in the same bed she had died in, even if he had changed the bedclothes. Martin couldn't afford to get a new bed. So, he had remained in his old bedroom that faced the garden, that he'd slept in ever since he was a child. He was glad of that now the girls had started tormenting him. Their voices didn't reach him here.

Martin sank onto the bed and stretched out on top of the tan and cream striped duvet, closing his eyes. He could still see the girls. All six of them. One with very white skin and red hair in a ponytail. One tawny-skinned girl had short black hair. Two possessed brown hair. One of them also had a ponytail. One had fair, almost white hair and the last was mousy blonde.

Why did they come to sit on his wall? There were other low walls in his street that they could sit on but they always chose his. They came every evening now, Monday to Friday. They were like vultures finding a fresh body to peck at. He shook as he thought about it. Of all the houses to pick in the road, they had to choose the one where the owner had a phobia about young girls or virgins.

He supposed that his tormentors were probably both. But then again, possibly not, seeing what he read in the newspaper about the younger generation.

•

He was running across green fields and even jumping over hedges and gates with ease. He loved this part of the dream. But then he became aware that grim-faced hunters were chasing him with blasts of a horn and flashing swords and cracking whips. They cornered him in a wood, and he couldn't get away. He backed against an oak tree, terror-stricken.

Martin woke up, gasping. He was slick with sweat. He reached across and took a big gulp of water from the glass on the bedside cabinet. It was dark, and the house creaked around him.

•

'Do the girls on the wall bother you?' Martin asked his next-door neighbours to the left when they answered the doorbell. The house on the right was empty, being refurbished.

'The girls on the wall?' Sandy and Mel stared at him.

Sandy was a black man, six feet tall with his black hair cut short. Mel was a short white woman with sandy coloured hair. Her name was short for Melanie so Martin understood why she had that nickname. He thought it hilarious that he was called Sandy and not her. She was much more a candidate for the name of Sandy than her partner. But Martin never commented on that. His mother had taught him it was rude to do that.

Martin tried again. 'The girls who sit on my front garden wall, don't they disturb you?'

'What girls?' Mel asked, raising her thin eyebrows.

'The girls who come every night and sit on my wall.' Martin heard his voice getting higher.

Sandy shrugged. 'Haven't seen them. But we've been away for months.'

'We've only just got back,' Mel chimed in.

Sandy and Mel stared at him.

Three months? How had Martin not noticed? Now, he thought about it, he realised that there had been a lack of activity next door. Although, to be honest, he hardly ever saw the couple, either of them. They were always away working or, if at home, keeping hours different from his. Martin didn't know what they did for a living. It was rare he nodded hello to them, let alone spoke to them.

'They sit there and shout and swear and drink. They're making my life a misery.'

'Sorry to hear that,' said Sandy, but he didn't look sorry.

'You should ring the police,' Mel said.

'You'll hear them tonight,' Martin told them.

It was only after he'd gone back inside that he remembered it was a Saturday and the girls didn't pester him on Saturdays.

•

Martin had his porridge before he rang the police. His mother had brought him up on having porridge for breakfast every day and he'd always thought it a good idea. He needed to fortify himself before the ordeal. Martin hesitated by the phone in the hallway. It was an old, sage green one, a landline that they'd had for many years. His mother had never wanted to get a cordless one. Too much chance of losing it down the sofa cushions, she'd said.

Should he ring 999 or the local station? He wasn't sure about the number of the local station, and he couldn't imagine the 999 operator being sympathetic with that information request. The latest Yellow Pages and Thomson Directories were so slim nowadays with so little information. Luckily, Martin had loads of them going back to the years when fat yellow volumes were produced. He went in search of one.

In the end, he decided to ring the station. He was convinced that the police wouldn't consider it an emergency even though he did.

The policeman's voice didn't sound friendly.

'I want to report something.'

'Can we start by taking your name and address, sir?' His tone was impatient.

Martin gave him these and then repeated, 'I want to report something.'

'Which is?'

'These teenage girls come every night and sit on the wall of my front garden.'

'So, you're saying, sir, that these girls come and sit on your wall.'

'My front garden wall,' Martin interrupted him, eager for him to remember all the details.

'Right, sir. And what do they do?'

'They shout, and swear, and smoke. And I'm sure they're drinking alcohol,' Martin said eagerly.

'What else do they do?'

Martin was surprised. 'Haven't I just told you what they do? Isn't that enough?'

'Do they come into your garden? Or have they verbally or physically assaulted you?' the police officer asked.

'No.'

'Have they put anything through your letterbox? Tried to set fire to your house?'

'No!' Now Martin had something else to worry about.

'Are they disturbing your neighbours? Do they accost people walking past?'

Martin hesitated before saying reluctantly, 'No.'

The police officer heaved a weary sigh. 'Then I can't see what you expect us to do about it.'

Martin was dumbstruck. He eventually managed to say, 'What do you mean?'

'What I mean, sir, is that I don't think we'd have grounds to even caution them. They're not trespassing…'

'They're sitting on my wall!' Martin protested.

'Yes, but the wall is the boundary between public space and semi-private space. They're not coming into your private space so they're not trespassing. They're not harassing you, they haven't assaulted or robbed you. They haven't vandalised your property. Teenagers don't have enough places to go, you know. We need more youth clubs and boxing clubs. They tend to congregate in public spaces.'

'My garden isn't public space!'

'As I said before, sir,' the tone was sharper now, 'a wall of a front garden abuts public space. At least they won't be getting up to any serious trouble when people can see them. Frankly, sir, we don't have the resources to deal with trivial matters like this. I suggest you simply tell the girls that they're bothering you and ask them to go away. I'm surprised you didn't try that first.'

'But…' Martin was completely unable to tell the police officer the true reason why he hadn't tackled the girls. 'There's six of them and one of me,' he blurted out but the police officer wasn't listening.

'Good day, sir, and thank you for your call.' The phone call was terminated and Martin was left staring at the phone in his hand.

•

Martin opened his front door a crack so he couldn't see the girls.

'Please go away,' he said. His voice sounded thin and trembling. This was no good. 'Please go!' he tried again. That was better. His voice was stronger.

'You talking to us?' Redhead asked. Her green eyes narrowed.

Martin swallowed. 'Yes. Go away. Go and sit on someone else's wall.' He'd forgotten to say please. 'Please.'

'Why?'

Martin was so annoyed; he opened the door further.

'You're always here, making a nuisance of yourselves.' He looked at the ground.

'We're not doing anything.'

'Yes, you are.'

'Come and make us.'

He couldn't tell who'd said that, but she sounded angry. Martin gulped. He'd hoped they wouldn't be confrontational. He couldn't stand being so close to them.

'Please go away,' he repeated and shut the door, relieved to have ended the confrontation.

He sank down on the sofa in the sitting room and sighed. What could he do? He faced endless evenings of this persecution. His only hope was when autumn made the nights draw in. He longed for autumn.

•

Martin was dozing on the sofa when a bang on the window startled him awake. He twisted round. As Martin twitched the sitting room curtain open, he got the shock of his life. He saw six faces pressed up against the window pane, distorted into inhuman shapes. He flinched and screamed. Their cruel laughter came through the glass. It was the girls. Martin slid off the sofa. Blinking at them, on his back like a beetle. They pulled back and guffawed then pressed their faces against the pane and banged on the glass again. He had told them to go away and instead, they were mocking him, by being in his front garden.

Martin turned over and pushed himself up as they jeered. Rushing from the sitting room. he found the phone. His stubby fingers dialled 999.

'Which service do you require, fire, ambulance or police?'

'Police.'

There was a few seconds' delay. *Hurry up, hurry up, hurry up!*

'Police. What's the emergency?'

'There are girls in my front garden, banging on the window.' The words tumbled out.

'I can't understand you. Please speak more slowly.' The operator's tone was gentle.

'Girls in my front garden. Faces pressed up to my window.'

'And? What else are they doing?' The operator didn't sound so gentle now.

'They're laughing at me.'

Martin could hear the operator take a deep breath. 'I'm sorry, sir, that doesn't constitute an emergency. Please get off the line and ring your local police station.' Her tone was cold.

'But...' Martin began.

'Please get off the line. Someone with a real emergency might be trying to call us. Otherwise, you could be charged with wasting police time,' she snarled.

Martin flung the phone from him as if it were red hot. It clattered against the side of the cabinet. After a moment of listening to the buzzing, he replaced the receiver.

He wasn't going to ring the police station, not after the cool reception he'd got before.

How he wished his mother was there. She wouldn't have taken any abuse from the girls. She would have driven them away with the broom. He could imagine her doing it. But his mother was dead and couldn't help him. No one was going to help him.

The girls were so close to him, only feet away. He shuddered.

Martin went up to his bedroom, his sanctuary. He curled up on the bed in a foetal position, knees as close to his large stomach as he could manage. Tears of fear and humiliation tricked down his cheeks.

How long was this torture going to continue? When the summer holidays started, the girls could stay there all day if they wanted. The evenings remained light for so long, they could be there until ten at night. Martin couldn't bear it.

•

The next day was rainy and blustery. The wind blew his large black umbrella inside and broke some spokes as he walked to the bus stop. Martin got off at the supermarket and went in to get some more supplies. This time, he bought only tins, goods that would keep. He needed to keep his stockpile high.

The rain lashed down as he scurried from the bus stop to his house. He fumbled with his keys. He was half drenched from the rain with his broken umbrella not sheltering him on one side.

He grew more cheerful once he got inside, changed, then stored his purchases in the larder. If he was careful, and didn't use them up too quickly, they would last him a good long while. The trouble was, he wasn't very good at rationing. If he had one biscuit, he always wanted another one. And another.

He was in the kitchen, debating whether to have one or two biscuits with his afternoon cup of tea when the front door creaked and there were footsteps in the hallway. Martin went into the hallway to investigate. To his horror, the front door was open and Brown Pony Tail was on the threshold, the other girls crowding behind her.

He'd forgotten to make sure the door was properly shut, and he hadn't put the chain on. Terrified, Martin fell back.

'You can't come in,' he whispered.

Brown Pony Tail laughed. So did the others.

She walked into his hallway and looked around.

'What a dump,' she said.

Martin bolted for the kitchen and slammed its door behind him. With luck, they would steal or vandalise and leave him alone. Then he could report them to the police and they would finally do something. The door handle jiggled as someone tried to open it. The kitchen door had always stuck.

With a loud crack, the door opened. Redhead entered, smiling, moving towards him, holding out her hand. On her palm nestled a red apple, of all things.

'Here, boy.'

Martin gave her one petrified look then turned and ran towards the open back door leading out into the garden. As he did, his body began to transform. He stopped.

His neck grew longer as did his ears. He couldn't see

properly. His arms grew down, forcing him to bend over until he was on all fours. All his clothes were rent apart by his swelling body and fell in tatters around his feet. They both shrank and widened. His shoes split in two and he kicked them off. The fingers on each hand merged into one and then turned yellow and hard. His feet did the same. They had turned to hooves. An agonising pain stabbed him in his forehead for a moment. Something odd was happening at the base of his spine. Then he felt long hairs brush his bottom and his legs, whisking to and fro.

He could see much further round to the side now but not right in front of him. He raised his head and then he could see a white horse with a long ivory horn reflected in the glass in the outside door to the kitchen.

Martin panicked. He ran towards toward the door. His horn hit the glass panel, smashed it, and thrust through, showering shards of glass over the tiled floor. The impact opened the door. He reversed and pulled his horn out. This scratched his horn but he couldn't feel it. He squeezed through the doorway with difficulty, scraping his side against the doorframe. It made a vase and a tub of shoe polish on the window sill clatter onto the floor.

·

Martin trotted out into the garden. He felt clumsy and awkward, unused to the size of his new body and the unfamiliar sensation of hooves. Then he cantered towards the fence at the far end of the garden. He had to escape. Martin tried to jump the wooden fence, but he only crashed through, breaking and splintering the panels and landed heavily on his side. As he looked up at the blue willow pattern sky, the girls arrived and clustered around him, laughing.

'Poor Martin,' Yellow Hair said, a compassionate note in her voice. She sat down beside his body, ignoring the nettles and brambles around. She lifted his head off the broken fence with some effort and placed it on her lap. Her serge skirt felt softer than the sharp splinters of wood and the brambles clawing into his flesh. Her soft hand stroked his mane, and he relaxed with the soothing motions. His frantic heartbeat slowed. They weren't going to hurt him.

'Look at me, Martin,' she commanded.

He couldn't help but gaze up at her. But once he was looking at her, he couldn't stop, her gaze entrapped him and in her eyes, he saw the reflection of his own great dark eyes.

He felt her other hand stroke the long horn jutting from his forehead. 'Such a beautiful horn,' she crooned, running her hand up and down its ridges. Martin didn't enjoy her doing that and shifted a little.

'No, no, don't do that. Keep looking at me,' said the teenage enchantress.

'Such a valuable magical horn,' said one of the other girls and the others snickered.

Martin felt a cold trickle of uncertainty about the girls' intentions run down his spine.

'All of a unicorn is valuable,' growled another one with a deeper voice, 'from their mane to the hooves.'

He was a unicorn. How could he have changed from a man into a unicorn? He thought about his mother's insistence that they keep themselves to themselves. Never make trouble, never cause a fuss, never be noticed. Be invisible. Had she been a unicorn too? Why had his mother never told him? Warned him outright?

The girls' laughter was harsh and unpitying as crows and it stirred dormant fears in Martin. Once again, he tried to move, to raise himself from the ground but Yellow Hair had hold of his horn and his mane and was pressing down. And now the other girls also pushed his hind quarters down when he moved them.

Then Martin felt a white-hot pain and felt hot blood gush out of his flank. He managed to pull his gaze away from Yellow Hair, struggled to raise his head, and looked around. A grinning Black Plait had a blood-stained cleaver in her hand and red liquid dripped off the sharp end. His blood. He understood then that they were going to slaughter him.

Then his head was tugged around and pushed to the ground by Yellow Hair. Black Plait moved to her side then raised her cleaver, ready to sever his horn from his head. As he watched aghast, she brought it down.

THE PERFECT HAM SANDWICH

Agent Foster tossed the transchronograph onto Theobald Willis' desk. It landed with a clang. Shocked, Theobald picked it up and checked for damage. The transchronographs were far too valuable to be treated in this way, but that was agents all over. Careless, especially Foster.

'It's broken,' Agent Foster said. 'Fix it, will you?' An order, not a request.

'What's wrong with it? Is it the chameleon field or the universal translator?'

'Overheating. Takes longer than usual to activate. You're the boffin, you find out. But I need it back pronto.'

With that, the tall, broad-shouldered man strode from the office. Theobald narrowed his eyes with dislike. Of all the agents, Foster was his least favourite. He was tempted to put it to the bottom of his to do list, but Foster was the golden boy of the agency. Theobald seemed to be the only one who didn't worship him. He knew this might have something to do with the fact that Foster was young, slim and good looking while Theobald was balding, fat and nothing to look at.

Theobald changed a couple of chips and oiled the clockwork mechanisms. Then his stomach growled, telling him it was time for food. He'd only had a bowl of dry-as-dust healthy muesli with bog awful soya milk for breakfast. Rabbit droppings would probably have had more flavour. But lucky rabbits weren't being monitored for their food intake and weighed weekly.

He glanced at the clock, only eleven o'clock, too early for lunch. But he had his secret stash of biscuits and cookies. Theobald hurried to his locker and pulled out a few packets, grateful no other technicians worked in the lab that morning. He noted the dwindling mound with concern. It was getting harder and harder to buy them. Then he concentrated on the immediate problem. A Jammy Dodger or a Milk Chocolate Digestive?

He selected a Jammy Dodger, tempted to take two but knowing he had to ration himself. The rules forbade eating or drinking in the lab. Theobald enjoyed sipping his mug of tea and the delicious jam of his biscuit. Unfortunately, he sprayed a few crumbs over the transchronograph but he tipped the device upside down to make sure he'd got rid of them.

Theobald fiddled more with the transchronograph until lunchtime. The Jammy Dodger hadn't done much to satisfy him. He was hungry but unenthusiastic about lunch options since the government had bowed to the large vegetarian contingent and slapped a tax on meat and meat products that put them well beyond the pay packets of normal people. He glowered as he thought about the agents, lucky bastards who could slip across to any alternative timeline they liked and gorge themselves.

The vision of a ham sandwich came to him, all thick-cut buttered bread and thick sliced ham, with yellow mustard oozing out of the edges. He could practically smell the mustard and the fresh white loaf. He salivated and licked his lips. Then he looked at the transchronograph with its green light blinking. It needed testing. If he used it to go to a timeline where ham sandwiches were easily available… well, he was only testing the equipment as per protocol.

He slipped the transchronograph onto his wrist; it resembled a large, bulky sports watch. He programmed it, estimating a timeline far enough away for the vegetarian movement not to hold sway, but close enough that a certain cafe nearby that used to sell ham sandwiches should still exist. Then he pressed the gold screw on the side.

Theobald had his doubts even before he went inside the place. He remembered it as 'Joe's Café', but the sign outside had been amateurishly altered with black paint to say, 'All American Deli'. Still, it was worth a try.

'What I want is a ham sandwich,' said Theobald in the crowded deli.

'Honey oat, whole meal, rye, mixed grain, flatbread, Italian herb and cheese, wafer thin ham, low fat ham, cold cut combo, pickles, lettuce, tomato, onion, sweetcorn, green pepper, cucumber?' The efficient young man in a sparkling white tee shirt, behind the counter asked the question without taking a breath. The holes in his ears were nearly closed up.

'Crusty white bread and I think thick cut ham, preferably

Wiltshire but it's not essential, oh and English mustard,' Theobald said.

'We can't do that.'

'Why not?'

'It's not patriotic.'

The deli assistant's gaze flicked behind Theobald who turned to see the posters on the wall, proclaiming in red and blue letters – THANK YOU UNCLE SAM FOR SAVING US and UK GOOD, USA BETTER.

Theobald snorted. 'Ridiculous.'

A hush fell. The customers stared at Theobald and inched away from him. The young man leaned forward. 'Listen, grandpa, have you been drinking? Do yourself a favour and pick something else.'

'No,' said Theobald in a huff and left the shop.

The transchronograph was definitely playing up. Theobald checked his instructions and the settings and tried again.

He didn't notice the two men in dark suits, sunglasses, with an earphone in one ear, who had followed him out of the deli.

They trailed him to a narrow alley. The first man nodded to the other, to hurry around to the other end. He saw the undesirable fiddling with a large watch and then, to his amazement, the undesirable melted into the air.

The other man hurried along from the other side of the alley.

'What the hell? Where'd he go?'

The first man frowned. 'Don't blaspheme.' Then, 'I have no idea.' He wasn't about to admit what he had seen and end up an undesirable himself.

Theobald emerged from the alley and went back to Joe's Cafe. Except it was now called 'Blondi'. The entire interior gleamed and sparkled from the glass display cases to the pine tables and chairs.

'What do you want?' the woman with aggressively blonde highlights asked, wiping the spotless counter down with a cloth.

Theobald repeated his request.

The woman stared at him. 'Wiltshire ham? We don't have that. Only Black Forest ham or Westphalian ham, the best in the world. And we only do open sandwiches with tomatoes, pickles or cucumbers. No exceptions.' She pointed to the board on the wall, then folded her arms.

Theobald sighed. As he turned to go, he noticed the framed photographs on the walls. The first showed a man with dark hair and a toothbrush moustache. *'Our Beloved First Fuhrer'*, the caption read. The next was a fat man with *'Our Beloved Second Fuhrer'*, and so on. He shivered and rushed out of the cafe, making for the alley.

The transchronograph was not working properly. He checked the settings and tried again.

'What would you like, monsieur?' asked a large man with an equally large moustache behind the counter of the café. The French Tricolour hung on the wall. There was a profusion of pastries in the display cases.

'What I want is a ham sandwich,' Theobald said.

The large man frowned. 'Monsieur would like a Croque Monsieur?'

'That's ham and cheese, isn't it? No, I just want a plain ham sandwich.'

'We do not have ham sandwiches,' the large man declared. 'We have Croque Monsieurs or Croque Madams.'

'Which are?'

'Croque Monsieur with oeuf on top.'

Theobald shuddered. 'Egg? No, thanks, I want a ham sandwich.'

'But that is impossible. We do not serve those. Our Croque Monsieurs are excellent. Even the valet to his Imperial Majesty, Napoleon the Seventh, comes here to our humble establishment for his Croque Monsieurs when he is in England.'

'I don't care if Old Harry comes here for one, I don't want one,' Theobald said. 'Good day.'

He left the shop mumbling to himself, 'Don't do ham sandwiches, what kind of lunatic asylum is this?' and bumped into a policeman with a bushy moustache and splendid golden epaulettes on his broad shoulders. The policeman growled as he pushed past.

'Apologise!'

Theobald looked back. 'Are you talking to me?'

'Indeed, I am, you cretin.'

'That's rich, coming from a moron in fancy dress.'

The man spluttered and lunged forward, grabbing hold of Theobald's arm. 'Insulting the Prefect of the Department of Paris.'

Alarmed, Theobald tried to shake the man's arm off.

'And now resisting arrest,' the man crowed.

This couldn't be happening. Agency staff had to blend in when they went to another timeline, not draw attention to themselves. And suppose they took the transchronograph off him? Frantic, Theobald turned a dial, no easy matter one-handed then jabbed the gold screw.

Phew! He was out in the open, but there was nobody around to witness his arrival. This time the sign read, 'Cleo's Wine Shop'. Not promising, but Theobald was too stubborn not to try. This time, a woman stood behind the counter in a long dress with a translucent veil over her hair.

'What can I get you?' Her voice was low and sultry.

'A plain ham sandwich,' Theobald answered without a great deal of hope in his voice.

She frowned. 'We can do you a plate of ham and olives and some slices of bread. What's a sandwich?' She turned her head and called, 'Lucius, ever heard of a ham sandwich?'

A tall thin man, in a blue tee shirt with a picture of a toga on the front, appeared through a doorway.

'No,' he said. 'What is it, something new from Nova Roma?'

'Do you have butter?' Theobald asked. He was willing to make the sandwich himself. Never let it be said that he wasn't flexible.

'Butter?' The woman stared. 'That's for burns, not bread.'

'Never mind,' said Theobald. His shoulders drooped. He left the shop.

He would have one more try, he promised himself, in

the grimy alley. Theobald fiddled with the settings and pushed the gold screw once again.

A pub with a sign, 'The Old Bull and Bush' beckoned him inside.

The pub was everything an English pub should be, dimly lit, comfortable chairs, a TV switched to mute, and customers talking in low voices as they drank. Everyone looked a little pasty to him, but it was probably the light.

The pretty barmaid had greeted him with a friendly smile that displayed her gleaming white teeth. Her hands were surprisingly cold when she passed him the pint.

'I haven't seen you before,' she said.

'No, I'm new here.'

Her beautiful smile was only marred by her two incisors being slightly longer than the rest but who was Theobald to criticise people's looks?

'That's nice. Welcome to our humble establishment. The sandwich won't be long.'

She brought it over quickly and set it down before him. Then she licked her red lips, an odd thing to do but who could blame her with such a glorious ham sandwich?

He sat in a corner with the sandwich and a pint of best bitter in front of him. He took another pull of the foamy beer, delicious, and lowered the pint glass. Then he reverently picked up one half of the crusty white bread doorstep, filled with a thick wedge of pink ham and bright yellow mustard trickling down the side. He bit into it. Fantastic. He devoured the first half and had another sip of his beer.

He wouldn't rush this wonderful gastronomic experience. Theobald didn't know when he would have another one. He looked at the transchronograph and realised with alarm that it was way past his allotted hour for lunch. Visions of being shouted at by his section head and Agent Foster filled his head. There would be hell to pay if they found out he'd been flitting from timeline to timeline. His pay would be docked with an official reprimand at the least and, at worst, he'd lose his miniscule pension.

'Why go back?' a little voice whispered to him. Theobald considered the idea. A world with ham sandwiches versus a world of unappetising vegetarian food. And where comfortably upholstered people like himself were subject to endless abuse and restrictions. And newspapers reported vegans were campaigning for the government to make milk and cheese illegal. He shuddered. That timeline would only get worse in his opinion. Or he could stay in this world that, despite their pale people and slightly disturbing barmaids, had perfect ham sandwiches.

His decision made, Theobald smiled and took another bite of his ham sandwich.

A MONSTER MET

'How about a picture?' the young, terracotta-skinned ship's photographer asked.

He was trying to ambush every group of passengers ambling past him along the hot, dusty dockside.

'No.' Joe swerved around him, towards the Constellation Orion. The huge, white cruise ship gleamed in the Miami sunshine.

'Oh, come on, wouldn't you like a memento of the start of your vacation?' the young man wheedled.

'I said no.' It came out as a snarl. Joe marched on.

The cool, dim interior was a welcome relief from the heat outside. He gave a small smile to the officer running his ship card through the machine. He had to be neither too happy nor too miserable, completely unmemorable.

'Welcome aboard, Mr Bouchard,' she said, smiling, and handed the plastic rectangle back to him.

'Thanks.' *Mustn't be rude either.*

Joe knew from experience it would be at least an hour before his luggage was delivered to his cabin. He'd go get something to eat at the buffet and then wander around the ship. Joe's smile broadened. The buffet was the start of the hunt.

•

Two crew members guarded the buffet, brandishing spray bottles of hand sanitiser. They squirted turquoise gel onto the hands of all the passengers they could catch. A sharp antiseptic odour filled the space. Joe disliked the feel of the gel so dodged them and moved forward. He washed his hands enough anyway.

The buffet area overflowed with passengers, all wanting their lunch and all desperate to find a free table. Joe, an old hand at this, selected a table where a couple of people already sat and asked if the other chairs were free. He marked his territory with the navy-blue napkins containing his silverware.

Appetising aromas wafted into his nostrils. The roar of conversation filled the air. Waiters flitted past, carrying drinks or trundling carts filled with dirty plates and silverware.

Joe got up to wander around after ordering a beer and paying with his ship card. Anyone observing Joe would have thought he was looking at the offerings at the sparkling food stations. Speciality of the day, pasta and pizzas, the roast meats, soups, salads, bread, desserts. It seemed like there were endless choices.

In reality, he was already scanning the crowds for that special one. Joe knew he was unlikely to find her so soon, but it never hurt to look. The Orion's wide corridors helped him move swiftly. He sidestepped and weaved amongst the passengers carrying plates piled high. Joe didn't find her, but he hadn't really expected to.

He had a whole ten days for his mission.

•

Joe had considered the possibility of a crew member but quickly gave up on that idea. His intensive internet research had showed it would be almost impossible for a passenger to go unnoticed in the crew quarters. And being unremarkable was one of his key assets. Pity, he'd rather have had a young, attractive woman.

He could have tried ashore, but he could foresee too many practical difficulties and a high chance of being recognised and/or remembered. No, it would have to be a passenger. His best bet was going to be a middle-aged woman.

Not all his victims were that age. He tried to vary it to stop being too easily profiled. The piles of True Crime magazines hidden in a closet at home had given him plenty of tips.

•

He didn't find her until the second day of the cruise. He'd had a few near misses. One plump American alone in the hot tub on the Aqua Deck had seemed promising, very friendly and giggly with no rings on her fingers but then her equally friendly and plump boyfriend plopped himself down beside them in the bubbles. Joe had a pleasant chat with them both about Dallas where they lived. He promised to meet them sometime for a drink, climbed out and melted away.

He sat by the pool at midday, drying off after doing a few desultory strokes. The pool wasn't big enough to do more than that and there were a lot of people in it. No one promising though.

The tannoy squawked that the Line Dancing Class was about to begin. A few women emerged hesitantly onto the dance floor in front of the pool, followed by a few more. Most wore vests and shorts, which looked better on some than others. Music blared out and the tall, slim instructor on the stage pranced about and yelled at them.

Then he spotted her.

She had her back to him. Her pink sundress billowed up, displaying her short fat legs. Her long blonde hair blew every which way. She made no attempt to follow the instructions but did her own thing and laughed with her fellow dancers as she did so.

Joe weighed the risk of people remembering the one man in the class against the chance to make an introduction. But there were plenty of balding men with bellies onboard. He had no distinguishing marks, no tattoos. Joe would reward himself with a tattoo as soon as he returned home after the cruise. He quickly finished drying himself off and slipped on his tee shirt.

Joe made his way onto the dance floor, moving to be next to her. An electric thrill went through him.

The hunt was on.

He danced next to her, exchanging glances and smiles. When the class finished, he followed close behind her. She stopped beside an old lady on a sun lounger. A Zimmer frame stood next to it.

'I'm going to get a frozen cocktail,' she told her.

'Can I have one too?' The old lady handed over her plastic ship card.

As she walked off, Joe heard the younger woman mutter, 'Don't bother to say please.'

She was British. Joe's heart hammered with excitement. She would be his first British one. And possibly more of a challenge as he hadn't met many Brits. He liked that. The last few killings had been too easy.

At the frozen cocktail stand, Joe slid in line behind her. After she gave her order, she turned around and Joe seized his chance.

'Sure is hot work, line dancing,' he said.

'More like an exercise class than line dancing.'

'I thought your dancing was great.'

'I wasn't really following the steps, more going freestyle.' She smiled.

'Well, your freestyle was great then.'

She widened her eyes in recognition. 'You were dancing too. Good for you.' She smiled at him.

'I'm Joe, by the way, Joe Bouchard.'

Joe had wondered whether to lie about his name but being on a cruise ship had altered the odds of being caught out in the lie. Besides, in his experience, people were usually pretty terrible with names. He held out his hand. She shook it. Good, firm grip.

'Pleased to meet you, Joe. I'm Ruby.'

'Ruby? That's a lovely name.'

In Joe's opinion, you never went wrong telling a woman she had a lovely name.

Her smile widened. He was proved right, just like Monica DeSalles in the park and Ava Graham in that bar.

'What'ya drinking, Ruby? Anything you'd recommend?'

'I'm having the Wildberry Margarita, but I haven't had it before, so I can't recommend it.'

'Had any of the others before?'

Ruby squinted at the menu on the wall. 'The Frozen Rum Runner, that's not too bad.'

'Good enough for me.' Joe ordered one from the none too friendly bartender who scowled at them. Most of the ship's crew were friendly and obliging but not this guy.

Joe strolled back with her between the long rows of sun loungers, full of passengers eager to make the most of the sunshine. Ruby handed one cocktail to the old lady who snatched it out of her hand and began guzzling the drink. Ruby rolled her eyes and sat down to sip her cocktail. To his delight, Joe saw an empty sun lounger next to her.

'Mind if I sit here?'

Ruby glowed. 'Of course not. This is Joe. He was in the dance class with me.'

'Pleased to meet you…'

The older lady stopped drinking long enough to say, 'Just call me Pam.' She smiled, oblivious to her cream moustache.

Ruby made frantic motions at her. When this didn't work, she leant towards her and hissed, 'Wipe your mouth.'

Pam grimaced and used the back of her hand. Classy. 'Honestly!'

Ruby unwrapped the paper napkin from around her glass and handed it to her.

'What can you do with them?' she asked, looking at Joe.

'Thank you, Ruth,' Pam said, emphasising the last word as she wiped her mouth again.

Ruby flushed a deep unbecoming red and looked daggers at the old lady.

So, Ruby's name was really Ruth. That told him a lot about her.

'Are you two sisters?' Joe asked to smooth over the tension. Nobody in their right mind could have mistaken them for siblings.

Pam beamed but Joe realised he'd made a big mistake from the appalled look on Ruby's face.

'I'm always being told I look young for my age,' Pam said, complacent.

Yeah, young for a hundred-year-old hippo. Does she never look in a mirror? Pam wasn't just fat, she was obese, with huge breasts dangling close to her vast stomach. Thank God, she wore a black sundress and not a swimsuit. At least she had long, pretty, glittering nails.

'Pam is my mother,' Ruby stated flatly.

'My mistake.' He winked at Ruby to let her know he'd been joking.

The frozen panes of her face relaxed. 'Where are you from?'

'Toronto.'

'I've never been. Is it nice?'

'It's okay.'

Ruby laughed. 'You obviously don't work for the Toronto Tourist Board. What do you do for a living, Joe?'

'Cab driver.' A job that was ideal for his alternative career. He saw their faces tighten. *Stuck up bitches.*

Ruby invited him to join them for lunch at the buffet. Joe was delighted. His patented nice guy persona was working.

•

Joe chewed over whether to go for Ruby or not. Pam was an added complication although he knew whoever he chose was likely to have a companion on board. An elderly mother might be easier than a friend or relative of the same age. The chances of coming across someone suitable in a single cabin was remote. The Constellation Orion only had fifty single ones out of 3,259. Joe had checked before he booked.

Ruby was the right age and type. She was divorced with no kids. She must have been pretty when young with her large blue eyes and button nose. Now, she'd put on weight and lines had been etched into her face. She must miss the attention from men she'd been accustomed to getting.

Joe did his best to find out all about them while revealing as little as possible about himself. Lucky for him, both Ruby and her mother liked to chat. In fact, they competed for airtime. They gave him little chance to contribute to the conversation whatever the topic.

•

When Joe approached Ruby and Pam two days later, he saw a man sitting on the sun lounger next to Ruby, chatting to them. The man was around his age, he supposed, stocky, with a head of thick grey hair and a sharp nose. Who was this interloper muscling in on his prey? Joe tensed with immediate anger then forced a smile on his face. Ruby looked up.

'Hi Joe. This is Godfrey.' She waved a hand at the man.

Godfrey stood up and shook hands with Joe. Joe deliberately squeezed his hand hard, but Godfrey didn't seem to notice. He sat back down, and Joe selected the empty sun lounger next to Pam. He sat down with a thud.

'Godfrey's from Bristol,' Pam said, eager to be part of the conversation. 'He's been on twenty cruises, fancy!'

Another Brit. This was not good. He and the women would have a lot in common. Joe didn't want or need competition. Maybe the man was just being friendly and would move on soon. No such luck. When Ruby invited Godfrey to join them for lunch later, Joe tried to hide his annoyance.

'I'm going back to my cabin for something,' he said.

'What've you forgotten?' Pam asked.

Nosey old bitch.

'My book.'

Ruby and Pam both looked surprised to Joe's increasing irritation. Figured he was too dumb to read books, did they? Not too dumb to plan and carry out over twenty killings without ever getting caught though. That took a cool brain, iron self-control and planning ability. Qualities that would come in very handy when carrying out an execution on a cruise ship. And walking away afterwards, scot free.

He went back to his tiny inside cabin and found the laxative powders in his washbag. He picked up a sachet and smiled.

Godfrey was disappointingly easy. All Joe had to do was to offer to get a couple of hot drinks after they'd eaten. Godfrey wanted a tea, just like a Brit. Joe slipped the powder into the white china mug and stirred it until it was completely dissolved in the hot brown liquid. After that, all he had to do was wait.

The laxative had promised it was fast acting on the box and it lived up to its promise.

Godfrey was lying on the sun lounger, talking about his roses when he jerked up and said breathlessly, 'Oh dear.'

'What's the matter?' asked Ruby.

Godfrey stood up abruptly. 'I have to go.' He farted loudly. He flushed. 'Sorry about that.' He farted again even louder. Godfrey set off at a run between the long lines of sun loungers.

Joe looked down at the wooden planks of the deck. He bit the inside of his cheek to stop himself from grinning.

•

Joe had thought long and hard about how and where to do it. His extensive online research had showed that cruise ships had CCTV cameras on all public spaces including elevators. So, no convenient dark corners on the decks. However, there were no cameras in passengers' cabins, so it would have to be Ruby's cabin.

Joe had intended to kill his victim the last night of the cruise. Then he'd found out that the crew collected the passengers' suitcases left outside their cabins from ten o'clock onwards. Too many people would be in the corridors. And too many passengers would be having an early night in their cabins. It would have to be the night before the end of the cruise. Irritating and it put him more at risk of being caught afterwards but nothing he couldn't handle.

The walk from the elevator to Ruby's stateroom would be monitored and recorded. He'd brought a plain black tee shirt, pair of pants and a baseball cap with no logo. He usually wore shorts so wearing pants would help to throw them off the scent. The pants had roomy pockets for the hard plastic ties and his trusty rope.

It was a pity he hadn't been able to bring any of his razor-sharp knives with him. He especially missed his favourite, Sharp Sammy. Ruby's death wouldn't be half so enjoyable. Still, he had the sharpened nail scissors. Joe had put them in his washbag to avoid detection. He'd be able to have some fun with those.

For a minute, he regretted choosing a cruise ship, it had certainly limited his options. Then Joe reminded himself that the murder was the thing, not how it was accomplished. And once he was inside the cabin, everything would be easy.

He needed to get hold of Pam's ship card, and to slip some Temazepam pills into her drink to make her woozy and sleep soundly. He knew he'd probably end up killing Pam as well. Unlike Ruby's death, that would be an annoying chore and he wasn't looking forward to it. He had been fantasising about Ruby's death, day and night.

•

Joe finally persuaded Ruby to come for a stroll around the Upper Deck with him after dinner the second to last night of the cruise. They stood looking over the railings, down at the black sea with the foaming white lines racing away from the ship.

'I love the sea,' Ruby said. 'I never tire of it.'

'Me too,' Joe said.

It was quiet on deck, far fewer people. There were many, tempting shadowy corners and dimly lit areas but Joe knew he had to resist doing anything other than kissing her. The cameras would be everywhere.

He pulled her into a corner, making sure she faced the cameras and not him.

Joe kissed her, a deep kiss that explored her mouth, as she twined her arms around his neck. She pressed her soft body against his. Her breasts rubbed against his chest. Joe's manhood hardened.

She moved her mouth away and kissed the left side of his neck, sucking at it. A love bite? Was she kidding? A sudden sharp pain. She had bitten him.

'Ouch!' Joe jerked away.

'Sorry, Joe, I guess I got carried away,' Ruby apologised.

Great. Now he would have a hickie like a lovesick teenager. He controlled his temper by imagining Ruby tied up and spread-eagled, awaiting his ministrations.

'No problem,' he said, trying to keep his voice calm and even.

Her mouth puckered. 'I'm really sorry.'

He obviously hadn't succeeded. Her blue eyes looked at him anxiously.

'Don't worry about it,' Joe said, a friendlier note in his voice this time.

She leaned forward and kissed him on the cheek. 'You're so sweet.'

Joe resisted the urge to rub her lipstick stain off immediately. She would be offended.

'Shall we go get another drink?' Joe asked.

Ruby yawned and put her hand over her mouth, looking shocked.

'I'm pretty tired. Sorry but I think I'm going to go to bed. It's really been a lovely evening, Joe. I'm so glad I met you. We must keep in touch. Are you on Facebook?'

'No.' No way he was putting any information about himself out on the internet. That was how people got caught.

'Oh, you really should.'

'I don't like the internet,' he said to shut her up. Not true, the internet had all sorts of uses for a serial killer.

She was giving him the brush off. All these come on signs and now, she was backing off. Just like all women. She deserved what was going to happen to her. She had it coming. At last! Joe controlled his jubilation. Not long now.

They parted to go to their cabins. Joe went back to his to change and get his equipment.

•

Joe walked down the corridor of the deck containing Ruby and Pam's cabin. It was near the end, so he had to run the gauntlet of the surveillance cameras the length of the corridor. He kept his gazed fixed on the red carpet patterned with yellow crescent moons and stars. He was wearing his baseball cap, so they wouldn't be able to tell if he had hair or not. He'd discard the black tee shirt and pants as soon as possible after tonight.

His eyes were troubling him. He screwed them up against the light. He pressed Pam's card against the small black panel by the door handle and it flashed green at the top. He opened the door just enough to allow him to squeeze through and not bring too much light into the room.

He paused to allow his vision to adjust to the darkness in the cabin. Dizziness overwhelmed Joe for a second and he swayed. Then he righted himself. It must be the excitement getting to him. Loud rasping snores came from the vast shape under the bedcovers in the bed nearest the cabin door.

Joe walked to the other bed with a smaller hump and bent down slightly. Ruby. She was lying on her back, unaware of what was going to happen to her. Excitement surged through him. Just as he felt in his pockets for the plastic ties, Ruby spoke.

'Well, hello Joe. Fancy meeting you here.'

For a second, he was paralysed. Then he lunged to hold her arms down and stop her from moving. He got hold of her wrists, but she pushed him off with a strength he'd never have believed she possessed. He tumbled to the floor, hitting his back, and she leapt out and stood by him.

He grabbed her ankle and pulled her down. How stupid she was to stand so close. She fell on top of him, and they struggled. He slapped her across the face but to his amazement, she didn't cry out or scream. Instead, she pulled her head back and head butted him. He felt a crack as his nose broke and blood spurted. Pain erupted. Fury filled him. He was going to tear this bitch into pieces. He reared up and heaved her away, so she fell backwards with a thud against the bedside cabinet.

Joe rose up. He wiped the blood away with his hand and pulled the nail scissors out of his shorts pocket. He would hurt Ruby real bad. He took a step towards her. Strong hands pulled him backwards and he was flung onto the carpet. Pam loomed over him.

'You don't play nice, do you, Joe?' she said.

Joe was stunned. How could she be awake with the number of Temazepam he'd put in her cocktail? He gaped at her.

She began to giggle. 'Not quite as clever as you think you are, Joey boy. It takes more than a few sleeping pills to knock me out.'

The blood ran into his mouth, making him gag. He spat it out and sat up. Pam grabbed hold of his head with both hands and smashed it backwards on the floor. The carpet softened the blow but not by much. Dazed and hurting, Joe lay there. Pam swung a foot and kicked him in the side. Her bare foot shouldn't have been able to do much damage, but it was a solid weight crashing into his ribs. He gasped.

'Mum! He's mine.' Ruby's voice was reproachful. 'Stop playing with him.'

'We can share,' was Pam's reply.

Ruby switched the bedside light on. She was wearing a low-cut negligee that left little to the imagination. She moved forward and leant down. The nighty dipped, and Joe got a good view of her beige pink nipples. Despite his agony, his cock twitched. Ruby noticed, smiled and then ground her foot into his crotch. The pain was excruciating. He started to scream and then her hand slapped over his mouth, reducing the sound to gurgles. Tears of pain trickled from his eyes.

Surely the passengers in the next-door cabin must have heard the noise. Why weren't they banging on the wall? Why weren't they doing something?

'No one's going to help you, Jo Jo. There's no one in the next cabin,' Ruby said as if reading his thoughts.

His throat was very dry, and his heart hammered. He tried and failed to move his feet. They were numb. To his alarm, he felt the same numbness in his arms. Paralysis crept through his veins. In a moment, he was unable to speak or move.

'Get on with it,' said Pam impatiently.

Joe begged Ruby with his eyes, as Suzette Villiers' large, dark eyes had beseeched him. Ruby ignored the silent plea, just as he had.

Ruby's face and figure began to shimmer and swirl until Joe could only see a blur of colours and lights. He blinked, and his vision cleared. He would have screamed but he was no longer able to. At least his eyes worked. He wished they didn't. There was a monster looming over him. She had tiny cold bird-like eyes, set in folds of flesh, a hooked nose and a wide mouth crammed with large, jagged teeth, sharp as daggers. She was naked. His appalled gaze dragged down long scaled arms to hands with long, yellow talons. Two small breasts were echoed by two more rows above a large, bare belly. Her feet had wicked looking talons too.

'Don't you like me anymore, Joe?' asked the monster in a grating voice. There was a harsh, cawing sound. It took a second for Joe to realise the monster he'd known as Ruby was laughing. The cacophony grew louder. The Pam monster was laughing too behind his back. He wanted to turn his head, but he couldn't.

'Bet you wish you hadn't spiked Godfrey's drink now. Eh, Joe?' the Pam monster asked in a horribly rough voice. 'We'd picked him as our meal, but you had to interfere.'

Meal? These bitches were crazy. Joe strained with every ounce of his will to move, to crawl away but he couldn't even move his big toe.

'Poor Godfrey was so embarrassed, he couldn't face us after that,' the Ruby creature chimed in. 'So, we had to choose someone else.' Her mouth stretched in a smile, showing her ugly teeth. 'Guess who we chose?

'You were so eager to be Ruby's friend.' Pam smirked.

The Ruby creature cawed with laughter again. 'To be my playmate.' She kicked him hard in the right arm.

Joe gasped. He felt a savage blow to his back and screamed silently with pain. Pam's turn to caw with laughter.

Joe stared up at the Ruby creature. What were they? Were they really going to kill him? How did they think they could get rid of his body without being discovered?

'I bet you've got lots of questions. What a shame you can't ask any.' The monster giggled, a horrible sound. 'Let's see, what do you want to know? We're not human, as you can see. This is our normal appearance. We can live under the sea or on land...'

'Why are you wasting time talking to it?' Pam interrupted. 'Let's kill it now.'

'Mum! Don't interrupt me when I'm talking.'

'You're not too old to get the back of my hand.'

'Don't embarrass me in front of our meal. Sorry about that, Joe. Let me see, where was I?'

Ruby, or the monster formerly known as Ruby, loved to talk. Joe hoped desperately that if she just went on long enough, someone would hear. Someone would burst through the cabin door and rescue him.

'Hoping the Seventh Cavalry will come to your rescue?' The monster cawed again. 'No one's coming.'

'They'll find nothing but your bones, Joe,' the Pam monster said. It cocked its head, considering. 'Apart from your blood, of course.'

Did they think they could just stroll out of the cabin, off the ship and away?

'I know what you're thinking, Joe. How will they get away with it?' the Ruby monster said.

The Pam monster cackled. 'We won't be here. We'll be long gone by the time the steward comes in. Over the rail and into the sea.'

Joe stared up at them. What were they? The Pam monster pulled back her leg and kicked him again. The pain reminded him he had more important things to worry about than what species they were.

'Dinner time,' the Ruby monster said, rubbing her hands.

Joe now understood the terror of his victims, knowing they were going to die. The helplessness. The loss of hope. He was struggling to breathe; his throat was closing up. His eyelids drooped shut. The last thing he saw were their jagged smiles. The seconds before blackness overwhelmed him were agony enough.

THE BOOM SHOW

I walk, legs like ironing boards, along the catwalk onto the stage. I am really going through with this. The quiz show host, Max Perry, turns to me as I blink against the bright lights of the lamps.

'And here's Contestant Number Six,' he purrs into the microphone.

The crowd bay their approval. They're pressed up against the Perspex fence that separates them from the contestants, the TV crew and the Bunker. From my viewpoint on stage, I can see the tiny group of protesters at the back with their huge LED Respect Your Elders badges flashing away. If you're watching the show at home, you can't see them. As if their protests ever do any good.

'What's your name, sir?' The audience like it when Max shows deference.

Close up, Max's skin is very taut and smooth. Not one line or wrinkle on his face and his saffron luxuriant hair is suspiciously even.

'George Appleby.'

'And where are you from, George?'

'The South London Stacks.'

'So, not too long a journey then to Teddington?' Max

smiles the complacent smile of someone who lives and works in one of the more exclusive areas of London.

'No, not too long,'

But scary, walking to the station in the early morning, ever watchful for lurking predators, conscious that running away is no longer an option with my arthritic knees.

And annoying, having to show my Ocard and I.D. card at every interchange to prove my right to travel on public transport.

And humiliating, having a full body search and mandatory shower once I'd managed to enter the hallowed enclosure of the studio.

'Are you feeling lucky, George?'

I've rehearsed for this. The fucking wishbone has been in the right-hand pocket of my jacket ever since my Last Supper. Feeling the smooth fragility between my fingers, I fight the urge to snap it. I pull the wishbone out of my pocket and brandish it for the crowd and the TV cameras' benefit.

'I sure do, Mr Perry, I've got my lucky wishbone, see?'

It's a nice touch, me calling him Mr Perry… shows I have old-fashioned values.

'Call me Max, please. So, it was roast chicken for your Last Supper, eh?' Max smirks. 'May I pull it with you, George?'

'Of course.'

I wonder what he would do should I refuse and toss the wishbone aside. I fantasise about shoving it up Max somewhere the sun doesn't shine. Now, that would be a novelty for the audience.

We each pull on one tip of the wishbone. Max's hand looks very pink and plump compared to my thin blue-veined hand. The wish bone splits and I keep the larger half. I admire Max's skill in ensuring that it happened that way. Of course, he practises every time someone chooses roast chicken for their Last Supper.

'What's your wish, George?'

I wink. I've been told the crowd and the audience watching at home like winks. 'Now, that would be telling, Max.'

The crowd roars.

See, I'm not senile; I can remember he's told me to call him Max. I would be a worthy winner, deserving a luxury lifestyle and all the medicine money could buy.

'Well, I think we can all guess, George.' Max turns to the crowd. 'Right, guys?'

There is an even louder roar of approval.

'Okay, George, time to get into your jacket and go to your seat. And George – stay lucky!' That's Max's catchphrase.

'I'll be lucky alright; I have my wishbone!' What a plucky contestant I am.

I wave it about to cheers from the audience and then do my best to walk briskly over to the waiting assistants.

A young, smiling woman helps me into the bomb jacket. The back has Number Six Sponsored By Time-

Warner-Virgin emblazoned in massive black letters on it. The front has the nice big red button. Easier for elderly, less agile fingers to press. She is a pretty thing, with glossy ebony hair and sparkling brown eyes. I know what Emmie would have said to her… 'Are you proud of the way you make a living?'

How we had despised The Boom Show in the comfortable years. But Emmie is dead and gone, the victim of teenager muggers on the lookout for elderly, therefore easy, prey in the Stacks.

As Max introduces the rest of the contestants, I imagine slamming the button on my jacket and stopping the murderous charade at once. Then it occurs to me with a sickening lurch. If I press the big red button, would it blow me to smithereens? Or would I be left looking like an idiot, vainly punching the button while the security guards rush to take me away?

An ear-splitting cheer erupts and alerts me it's time for the show to start.

'Contestants to your stands, please.'

We stand up and shuffle to our places except Contestant Number Twelve an old Asian woman with a neat grey bun, looking very colourful in her red sari under her yellow bomb jacket, who wheels herself to a specially lowered stand. Asians don't love their elders more than anyone else, that's a myth. A single red rose lies across her lap. What's so lucky about a red rose?

'Now, we all know the rules but just for you old timers, I'll repeat it again. We'll call two contestants. I will read a question out. Whoever presses the buzzer first and says the correct answer, wins.' Max flashes a smile at the cameras. 'The loser will be eliminated from the round. He or she will then go to the Bunker.' Max looks appropriately grave. 'The game continues until there is only one person left. Tonight's winner. Any questions?'

There are no questions. Everyone, contestants and audience alike, has seen The Boom Show hundreds of times before.

'Stay lucky!'

This is the perfect moment. My finger hovers over the button and then my hand falls to my side. Why not wait to see how it goes? If I lose, I can always try it then and see if it works.

They call Numbers Two and Three.

'Who was the last female monarch of Great Britain who reigned in her own right?'

Number Two is too slow. Three answers the question, pounding the button on the stand with his fat, balloon-like hand.

'Queen Elizabeth the Second,' he shouts.

'Correct, Harry, you remain in the game. Coral, I'm afraid you've lost and must go to the Bunker.'

Two, a black woman with hair so white and fluffy it makes me think she has a thousand dandelions planted on her head, says nothing. Her shoulders droop as she walks off the stage and starts down the long gangway on the left that leads to the heavy metal doors of the Bunker. Two large, armed guards escort her, supposedly a guard of honour. There is silence as the doors automatically open and swallow her up. A few moments later, a faint boom sounds from inside the Bunker.

We've all signed documents saying that we'll kill ourselves if we lose, that makes the show legal. Only now does it occur to me that perhaps, once behind the gates, your death might not be so voluntary.

Eleven to go.

'On with the game,' says Max, who has replaced a momentary serious look with a big grin on his face.

By the time my turn comes, there are five contestants left. They've had two commercial breaks to raise the tension. I stand, looking at Max. My legs ache. Rivulets of sweat run down my chest and my hands are clammy. My finger rests on the button.

'Where is the Hudson River?'

My finger jabs the button, but I am too late. Number Seven has got there first.

'North America,' Seven trumpets, a very tall, thin man with a fringe of curly grey hair around his pate and a monster moustache.

'Could you be more precise?'

'Canada.'

'I'm afraid that's wrong, Ray. George, can you answer?'

'The USA,' I croak.

'What was that, George? Loud and clear, please.'

'The USA,' I repeat in a stronger voice.

'That's right!' Max seems delighted. 'Ray, you gave the wrong answer. George answered it correctly, so George wins this round.' His voice pitch drops a little. 'Ray, I'm afraid you must go to the Bunker.'

Ray glares at me and then stomps off the stage on to the gangway, bumping into a guard and tripping as he does so. Both guards grab him by the arms to steady him, but then keep their grip on him all the way to the Bunker's doors.

That so easily could have been me. My stomach hurts as if someone has punched me in the gut. I'm no martyr. I don't want to die, I want to win. I thought there was nothing left to live for with my Emmie gone and my terminal illness, but the threat of death has shown me that being able to breathe and think is enough. I'd be happy to settle for the hand-to-mouth existence I endure in the Stacks.

Four left.

Yet another commercial break. The producer allows us to relax in our chairs for ten minutes. I scrutinise my opponents with more interest now. Number Twelve, the old woman in the wheelchair, is smiling. Number Nine is another tiny woman with a wizened face, she looks to be the eldest of the group; she seems worried despite her splendid performance. Number Eleven is a very good-looking, older man with a full head of wavy, silver hair. He oozes confidence.

I'm sure the rumours are true… they hand pick which contestants survive the longest. It's no coincidence they haven't called me until late on. I wonder why I am a favourite; perhaps my sad story or my brief chat with

Max earlier had helped. It doesn't matter why. Now, if I keep my nerve, I could win. I must be quicker. I can't rely on another contestant making a mistake again.

They call Nine and Eleven. Nine loses and stumbles off, weeping. This time, it really seems like the guards are helping her to keep upright while walking down the gangway to the Bunker. Another faint boom sounds.

Only three to go.

The smell of gunpowder increases in intensity after every round.

'Number Six.'

That's good, Eleven should be a little more worn out from the previous round. I look at him. The bastard just looks elated from his previous win, not sorry at all about poor Nine.

'Okay, contestants, fingers poised. What is the largest land mammal?'

My finger hits the blue button hard, a fraction of a second before Eleven's does.

'Elephant!' we both chorus.

Max listens to his earpiece. I'm sure I hit the button first, but will they agree? I want to scream, 'Me! I was first! Me!' but I stop myself. It might sway them to pick Eleven.

At last Max speaks. 'Okay. It's confirmed. George just beat Kelvin to the button so… George is the winner. Kelvin, I'm afraid it's now your turn to go to the Bunker.'

Kelvin's face crumples and he sags, his self-confidence leaking out of him like a pricked balloon slowly losing its helium. I should feel sorry for him, but I'm so relieved that I can't spare any pity for my fallen adversary. Minutes later, a distant noise comes from inside the Bunker.

Two left.

Number Twelve and me. I give her a quick glance. I don't like her composure. She should look scared or worried or pleased, but her face betrays no emotion. Her hands rest on her lap with never a twitch or tremble.

Another bloody commercial break. Some of the audience chant, 'George!' but others shout, 'Uma!' Vultures, ghouls, this is the modern-day equivalent of a hanging and don't the crowd enjoy it. I could still blow myself up, but I'm so close to winning, I can almost taste the champagne.

'Welcome back to The Boom Show, the most popular quiz show in Britain,' Max says into his microphone.

I lever myself up off my chair and limp to the stand. I'm tired. All this pressure is getting to me. Only one more to go.

'Right, George and Uma, this round will decide tonight's winner so listen carefully to the question.'

Bastard. As if we don't know this is the final and one of us is only minutes away from death.

'Who won the 2018 World Cup?'

They've decided I'll win, I think with joy as my finger hammers the button. A vision of last week's grinning winner appears to me. He'd been in a wheelchair. They can't allow a disabled person to win two weeks in a row. It would expose the fact that the show is rigged.

'Brazil!' I yell.

'Absolutely correct, George!' Max crows before putting a solemn expression on his plastic face as he turns to Twelve. 'I'm afraid Uma…'

She cuts across him. 'I know, Max, it's my turn for the Bunker. Congratulations, George.' She smiles at me.

My pleasure evaporates. The cow, how can she smile at me like that when she knows that she's going to her death? An impulse comes to me, to cry out, 'I don't want to win, let Uma have it instead.' But the icy suspicion Twelve said exactly that to make me feel guilty and give up the prize, stops me. Fat fucking chance. I've endured The Boom Show and won, and I damn well deserve a lifetime of ease and luxury for the rest of my months.

A guard wheels away Twelve. Shortly afterwards, I hear the last faint bang of the evening.

One left. Me.

I've won.

A TALL TREE TALE

'Do you know why you're here, Malcolm?' asks Detective-Sergeant Harris, the senior of the two detectives facing him across the table, a hard-faced woman with salt and pepper hair.

'No.'

'We received a Missing Person's Report about your wife from a family member. Interesting that you didn't report her missing.'

'She isn't missing.'

'Oh really? Do you recognise these, Malcolm?' She gestures to the table. On it lie a pink leather passport holder… the gold crest worn and faded, a Barbie-pink fake leather purse and a mobile phone with a cover patterned with pink roses.

'Yes, they belong to Joely,' he mutters.

'A little louder for the tape please, Malcolm.'

He raises his voice. 'They belong to my wife.'

'And they give us a problem. If, as you say, your wife stayed behind in the USA when you came back from your holiday, why are they in your possession?' she asks.

'I didn't want to leave them behind for anyone to find.'

The detectives exchange a glance.

'Is your wife alive, Malcolm?'

'Yes!'

'But wouldn't she need her passport and credit cards?'

'And I'm sure she'd want her phone,' Detective-Constable Grey chimes in.

'And why haven't the police in New England been able to find her, Malcolm?' DS Harris asks.

'It seems that nobody has seen or talked to your wife for a few days before you came home. So, what happened, Malcolm?' DC Grey asks, keeping up the pressure.

'Did you kill her, Malcolm?' DS Harris asks.

'No! I loved my wife,' he says.

He said loved, not love, she notes.

He looks DS Harris full in the face. Has he heard that liars can't do that? He's wrong. Next, he will be offering to shake my hand in a firm grip, she thinks.

'What's happened to her?'

Malcolm is silent for a moment, then sits up straight and says, 'What I'm about to tell you sounds unbelievable but it's the honest truth.'

The two police officers lean forward.

'Try us,' DS Harris says, her tone inviting. She feels her heart beat faster in anticipation... is he about to confess?

Malcolm gazes across at the wall, seeing somewhere else other than the green-painted wall. He looks as if he's no longer in the narrow interview room that smells of disinfectant, sweat and cigarette smoke.

'We stopped to take some photos of the trees. That's why we'd gone to New England in October, to see the leaves changing colour, the Foliage Trail they call it. Joely loves trees. She belongs to the Woodland Trust.'

'Was it an accident?' DS Harris coaxes.

'She'd picked up a maple leaf and she was looking at it on her palm. I turned my back to take some photos. That's when it happened.'

'What happened?'

'She turned into a tree.'

They both stare at him.

'She called my name and I turned round. Joely'd walked into the wood and was standing amongst the trees. She raised her arms into the air like she was stretching. Her skin became dotted with green and brown, which spread into patches. The patches linked up until she was totally green and brown.' He chokes then continues, 'She grew taller and taller, and her arms split and split again to become branches and her fingers turned into twigs that sprouted leaves. Her legs split, became roots, and slithered into the ground. Her face was the last to melt away. Then red and golden leaves appeared on the branches. She turned into a tree.' His voice grows stronger by the end and is full of conviction.

'Excuse me?' the two detectives chime together.

'She became a tree.' He looks pleadingly at the two. 'I know it sounds crazy but it's the truth.'

'You expect us to believe that?' DS Harris asks but she is troubled; Malcolm's body language is not that of a man telling a fabricated story.

'I have a photo.'

He fumbles in his pocket, pulls out a black iPhone, taps in the code, scrolls through the photos, and offers it to her. DS Harris grabs it and both detectives look at the photo. It is a grainy blur of grey, brown, and green. There is a slight trace of pink towards the top of the photo.

'I didn't think about videoing her until it was too late,' Malcolm says, shaking his head.

DS Harris scrolls onto the next picture. It is of a tree with a heart and the initials MM and JM carved low on the trunk.

'You're telling us your wife turned into a tree and you carved your initials on her?'

'So, I'd recognise her,' Malcolm pleads. 'I didn't like carving into her, I was worried about hurting her if... when she turns back but I needed to recognise her again. The trees all looked pretty similar.'

'Why didn't you just tie something round the tree?' DC Grey asks.

'There was nothing to tie around it,' Malcolm explains, 'and I didn't do it straightaway. I came back every day for a week to see if she would turn back. I kept getting funny looks from the other people who stopped but I waited every day until sunset. She didn't turn back.' His voice breaks.

DS Harris scrolls back past the blurry photo to a picture of Malcolm and Joely with their arms around each other, smiling at the camera. Joely has long red hair and freckles.

'What really happened, Malcolm?'

'I told you. You have to believe me. I don't know why it happened. Why her? Why me?' He stops and stares down at his shaking hands.

They take him through his story again and again. It never varies.

After the last recital, DS Harris asks, 'What did she do, Malcolm?' Her voice is soft.

'I've told you… she walked into the wood and turned into a tree. She's still there. I know you think I killed her, but I didn't. You have to believe me!' His voice rises and he bangs on the table. The two police officers tense.

'Calm down, Malcolm. Interview terminated at eleven o'clock a.m.,' DS Harris says abruptly and switches off the tape recorder. She nods at the constable standing by the door, 'Take Mr Miller to a cell please.'

'No! You have to believe me! She turned into a tree,' Malcolm bellows even as the constable takes him by the arm and hauls him out of the room. They can hear his shouts gradually getting fainter.

Once the shouts have stopped, they look at each other.

DC Grey blows out a breath. 'And I thought I'd heard them all!'

'There'll always be something new on The Job, Sam,' DS Harris advises from her years of experience. 'As I see it, there are two possibilities. One, he killed her and he's trying it on, and two, he's delusional. For my money, he's delusional; he thinks he's telling the truth. Murdered his wife and can't accept he's done it. No point carrying on with the interviews until we get a psychiatric evaluation.

The quacks will tell us which it is. Let's go report to the guv'nor.'

'He's having us on,' DC Grey says with conviction.

'You may be right. But you'd think he'd come up with a better story than that. A woman turning into a tree!' DS Harris snorts. 'What a preposterous idea! My money's on he's round the bend.'

THE YOUNG WOMAN
IN THE YELLOW BIKINI

She wore a yellow bikini. Every time. And it reminded me of that song, 'Itsy Bitsy Teeny Weeny Yellow Polka Dot Bikini'.

On our first night at the Les Espadrilles Resort on Antigua, we went for teppanyaki at Kimono's. Spaces for twelve people around a large square metal table/cooking area. The couples who were already seated were young, American, excited, talking about their honeymoons. There was only one other couple over thirty.

'Let's sit next to them,' my husband Neil murmured.

When they opened their mouths, we realised they too were British, making for an instant bond. We talked and joked with them before the chef's arrival. He deftly diced the food with his sharp, gleaming knives and seared the mounds of pink shrimp, rose pink salmon and scarlet steak in front of us.

Afterwards, the four of us walked through the darkness, the only lights low down amongst the black shapes of the plants. The night was loud with the sound of cicadas. We ended up in the piano bar, up the spiral staircase in the main lobby. The darkened piano bar was cosy and intimate. An old black man at the piano played his tunes while we drank and chatted. I felt a little sorry for him because no one was listening to the music.

Although around our ages, Dean and Debbie Charteris were on their honeymoon.

'Are you on your honeymoon too?' Dean asked.

'Us? No, I got the ball and chain years ago.'

'Is this your first time in Antigua?' I asked Debbie, to change the subject.

'Yes for me. No for Dean.'

A little pause then Dean blurted out, 'No, I've been here before with my first wife.'

I couldn't think of anything to say to that and neither, I suppose, could Neil. I wanted to raise my eyebrows at Neil but restrained myself.

Tequila Sunrise followed Singapore Sling followed Pina Colada, very easy to do when they are all free. Dean and Debbie were knocking them back and Neil was doing his best to copy them.

'The bar is open till two a.m.,' I pointed out to Neil, seated next to me, looking more than a little bleary-eyed.

'Oooh, the missus keeping tabs on you, is she?' Dean asked.

'She knows better than that.'

Neil tensed beside me.

'Sorry,' I said to him. 'You're on holiday, have as many as you like.'

'I don't need your permission,' he snarled then laughed as if it was a joke.

Dean laughed too. 'That's the spirit,' he said. 'Can't let the little woman get the upper hand, can we?'

Debbie swatted him playfully, 'I don't hear you complaining in the bedroom.'

He laughed again. 'Time to visit the loo. Get me another Harvey Wallbanger, would you, Debbie?'

Neil and Dean both disappeared off to the toilets at the same time. Debbie leaned towards me, her face flushed. Her dress was low cut, displaying her large breasts almost restrained in a black lace bra.

'Dean doesn't like to talk about his first wife,' she hissed confidentially. 'But he keeps a photo of her in his wallet.'

'Did they divorce or…?'

'Drowned,' said Debbie bluntly. 'It was an accident, here at this very resort.'

'Oh my God! How sad.'

'Wasn't it? It's taken Dean years to get over it. He said he wanted to come back here for closure and to make a fresh start.' She smiled a self-congratulatory smile.

Good luck with that. Neil is always going on about Lucy, the wonderful girlfriend he had before me

'I think I've made him forget all about Julie,' she said and giggled.

The men returned at that point which put paid to that conversation. Before we left the bar, we agreed to meet the next day at the main swimming pool.

•

'You can take your shirt and trousers off, you know,' said Debbie. 'I can't see you getting burnt under cover.'

She was definitely uncovered, wearing a halter neck black and white bikini with a bow at the front of the bikini top. Half moons of her breasts were clearly visible and her stomach was rather rounded but she obviously did not care.

'I will in a bit,' I assured her, smiling, trying very hard not to look at Neil.

Debbie and Dean splashed into the pool, calling to us to join them for a swim to the bar.

I looked at Neil.

'Do you want to go for a swim?' Asking for permission.

'You go for a swim, if you want to. I'm reading my Kindle.'

He was very proud of his new Kindle Voyager. He made a big deal every day of getting it out of the beach bag and turning it on. He didn't realise that no one would pay any attention as so many people round the pool had Kindles.

I slipped out of my long, loose shirt and trousers I had on over my black swimming costume with long legs, and waded into the water. I never wear bikinis, I hate the sight of my concave stomach. I swam across to Debbie and Dean, perched on the stone mushrooms by the bar. I ordered a Pina Colada. The bar attendant quickly placed the drink on the stone bar. I thanked her and reached up to get the cocktail.

'That's a nasty, big bruise on your forearm. How did you get that?' asked Debbie.

'I slipped in the shower. Silly of me.'

'You want to put some Arnica cream on that,' she advised. 'Have you got any here?'

'Yes, thanks.' I always carried Arnica cream around with me.

I saw the girl in the yellow bikini for the first time at the main swimming pool. She was sitting on a sun-lounger, under the stone colonnade near us. Her bikini's jaunty yellow colour was a sharp contrast to the expression on her face. She looked as miserable as a lobster in a boiling pot. She was young, early twenties with short blonde hair and was rather plump. I could clearly see her potbelly. I wondered why she wore such a revealing bikini when there were all these slim, tanned, attractive bodies around her. I smiled sympathetically at her but her protuberant blue eyes looked straight through me. Annoyed at such unfriendliness, I looked away. I felt quite irritated with her. If I could manage to enjoy myself in Antigua then so could she. What did she have to worry about?

The odd thing was, I didn't see anyone talk to the young woman or her speak to anyone, all the time that we were there by the swimming pool. She lay on the sun-bed, not sipping a drink, not reading a book, just sulking. Eventually Neil suggested that we go back to our room to get ready for dinner and I forgot about her.

'Ask for a slip mat for your bath,' yelled Debbie after us as we started trudging back.

'Mind your own business,' Neil muttered. He looked at me. 'What have you told her?'

'Nothing. She noticed my bruise.'

'I hope we don't see too much of them.'

I looked at him in surprise. 'I thought that you liked them.'

'Not me. He's boring and she's just an annoying busybody.'

•

The next day, Neil suggested that we stay by the small swimming pool next to our apartment. He went down to put towels on the loungers and I stood on the balcony to see how many sun-loungers were taken. Just then, Dean and Debbie came into view.

'Found you!' called out Dean, beaming at Neil.

'We didn't see you at the big pool then clever Dean remembered your block and room number.'

I didn't dare look at Neil.

'You don't mind us joining you, do you?' asked Dean.

'Of course not.' They didn't notice it came out through clenched teeth.

Dean and Debbie helped themselves to loungers. The young woman in the yellow bikini also strolled into view and sat down under an umbrella. She lay very still on the lounger, her face turned towards the foliage, taking no notice of our conversation.

She was always there when we went to the swimming pool. Was she stalking us? Although I never saw her once darkness fell with Caribbean abruptness, not in any of the restaurants nor the shows.

'I wonder if she's living off pizzas from the takeaway pizza bar, in her room, and that's why we never see her in the restaurants,' I said to Neil a few days later while we were getting ready to go out to dinner.

'What on earth are you talking about?' he asked.

'You know, that girl who's usually at the pool as the same time as us, the fat, fair haired one in the yellow bikini.'

'I don't know what you're talking about. Never seen her.'

'You must have done.'

He stepped up to me, so close I could feel his breath. It smelt of mint toothpaste.

'Stop it. I said I hadn't seen her and I haven't. You're starting to annoy me and you know what happens when you make me angry.'

I did know so I shut up.

•

The next day we met Dean and Debbie at the beach. Neil had become resigned to them constantly joining us. There was a low wall between the resort and the golden beach. Uniformed security guards monitored the gaps between the wall to keep the vendors from pestering the guests too much.

Dean and Debbie levered themselves off their loungers.

'Where are you off to?' Neil asked.

'We're off to sign up for the free snorkelling. Are you two planning to go?'

I shook my head.

'But you should, it's great fun, isn't it, Debbie?'

'I don't know, I've never been but I'm dying to try it.' She smiled at Dean.

'Free snorkelling,' repeated Neil. 'Yes, we could try that. If it's free.'

'Oh, it definitely is,' Dean assured him.

'I'm not sure I fancy it,' I dared.

'Rubbish. You shouldn't be so wet. Do you good to try something different.' I could tell from the note in Neil's voice there was no point trying to argue with him so I gave in.

I had been watching the local vendors for the last few days. I felt sorry for them as they didn't often have a taker on their offerings. Neil had gone to get us a couple of cocktails. Now was my opportunity to buy something without him creating a fuss. A black woman with short hair threaded with grey and carrying a large colourful shawl, full of goods, over her back, stopped on the other side of the wall.

'Afternoon,' she said. 'Having a nice day? Where're you from?'

She was trying the friendly approach but I didn't have time for that. My beach bag could hide something small.

'What jewellery have you got?'

She looked taken aback at my abruptness. I felt the need to explain.

'I'd like to buy something before my husband comes back.'

Her grin contained one gleaming gold tooth. 'Likes to keep a tight grip of the purse strings, does he? Let's see what I've got for you.' She unloaded her shawl and spread it out on the stone wall, displaying the goods to me.

'The turquoise necklace.'

The transaction was quickly over. I should have haggled. The price was rather high but I wanted to make sure that Neil did not know about it. It was my revenge for him making me go snorkelling.

The girl in the yellow bikini was under the next palm umbrella. The woman walked towards her, halted then took to her heels, her bundle banging against her back as she ran. I was still staring after the running woman when Neil returned, bearing two large Pina Coladas.

'What's up?' he asked.

'Oh nothing.'

His eyes narrowed. 'Did you buy anything from that woman?'

'No.'

He had the drinks in his hands so that stopped him from going through my bag and then luckily, he forgot all about it.

•

An hour later, we were on the swaying boat, listening to the man instruct us about snorkelling in the sea. Dean and Debbie didn't pay any attention; they fussed with their safety jackets and snorkelling masks which was rather rude of them. Then I saw the girl in the yellow bikini. I hadn't noticed her when we were assembling by the hut for snorkelling. The odd thing was she wasn't wearing the regulation safety jacket or the flippers or a mask.

'So, go have a great time, snorkelling,' the instructor finally said, 'and hey, remember, avoid the jellyfish. There seem to be a few around today.'

We all took it in turns to clamber down the steps, no easy matter when wearing flippers that made you twice as clumsy as usual. I looked back once I had splashed into the warm green water and saw the girl in the yellow bikini still on the boat. That explained why she wasn't wearing a safety jacket but why had she come along then?

I put the plastic mouthpiece into my mouth and took a deep breath. I put my face into the sea. Fish of all colours were swimming along, below me. I began to follow them. I was enjoying myself when screams split the air. There was a commotion about twenty yards away, two heads bobbing up and down. A voice calling, 'Help! Help!' Debbie's voice.

Two men jumped off the boat and swam to the noise. Three heads bobbed about and then there were two men pulling a man's body aboard the boat.

A voice boomed, 'Everybody, please make your way back to the boat now. Get back to the boat now!'

Dean had been stung by a swarm of jellyfish. The crew were carefully pulling strands of tentacles off him. His moans seemed to pluck at my nerves and set them jangling. I bit my lip.

'I hope they carry something for jellyfish stings otherwise they're going to pee on him,' Neil told me. 'Urine stops the pain.' His eyes sparkled.

'Not in front of everyone?' I was shocked.

But one of the men produced a tube of cream, to Neil's disappointment. The moans stopped. Then Dean cried out, clutched his right arm and his head fell back. One of the crew shouted out, 'Is anyone on board a doctor?'

Everyone shook their head.

'What's happening?' Debbie asked, her cheeks striped with tears.

'He's fainted. Don't worry, ma'am, we'll get him to a hospital as soon as we can.'

Everyone looked upset and worried, everyone except the girl in the yellow bikini. I caught her smiling and turned to Neil, shocked.

'Did you see that?' I demanded. 'There's poor Dean in agony and that girl is smiling as if it's a big joke!'

I was so angry, I started to struggle across the boat to give her a good ticking off. But somehow, what with trying to keep my balance and weave between the passengers at the same time, by the time I reached her side of the boat, she'd disappeared. She'd probably clocked my angry face and gone below to escape me. In the commotion of getting Dean into the waiting ambulance, I forgot about her. Debbie went with him to the hospital in St John's, the capital.

•

Dean died late that night. Apparently, he'd had a heart attack as a result of the stings. Debbie sobbed the news to us the next morning. Neil put his arms round her to comfort her and from then on she clung to Neil. I tried not to be irritated by her behaviour; she had just lost her husband after all, and instead tried to make myself useful. Debbie cried all the time, she didn't seem able to do anything for herself.

'Please don't leave me,' Debbie begged, long black trails of mascara down her cheeks. 'Could you pack up Dean's things? I can't bear to touch them.' And she burst into tears. Again.

'You do it, Emma. I've got to look after Debbie.'

I was packing up Dean's belongings and asked, 'Where's Dean's valuables and documents?'

Debbie said, 'Why don't you try looking in the safe? His passport, driving license and wallet are there.' She gave me the code and for some reason, this brought on a fresh shower of tears.

I opened the room safe and found his wallet and passport inside. I opened his wallet to check the contents, and caught sight of a small photo, underneath the transparent cover of a side pocket. It was of a plump young woman with short, blonde hair. I stared at it for a long time. I recognised the face. I had seen that smile on the boat the day before. The girl in the yellow bikini.

•

The next morning, I got up early, went outside onto the balcony and looked down. The swimming pool was half in dark shadow and the umbrellas were still down. The birds were chirruping in the moss green and viridian, luxuriant foliage. The girl was already there, lying on a lounger. The left side of her hair and head was covered with blood and she drooped toward the right.

I clutched the rail of the balcony. I froze. She looked up. For the first and last time, she actually looked at me, her left blue eye a vivid contrast to the scarlet blood streaking her face. My heart hammered in my chest. She stared for a long, terrifying moment and then she was gone, popped like a burst bubble.

Had she been haunting Dean? He wouldn't have mentioned he was seeing the ghost of his dead wife. Especially, as I was now sure her 'accident' had been no such thing. But you'd have thought it would have shown in his behaviour. He had seemed perfectly fine to me. And why was she haunting me? Then I understood.

I never saw her again. I left Neil two days after we got back to England.

MOONSLEEP

Edmund was on a boat sailing to the moon. As the boat began its slow descent down to the moon's silvery surface – it sparkled like snow on a sunny day – upturned faces pale as the moon stared up at him, shouting, 'Edmund!'

He woke up.

'Edmund, wake up, Edmund!' It was his master's voice. He turned to face him.

Master Zeale sat up on the other pallet. 'The spell worked. I've broken the curse.' There was a gleeful note to his voice, one Edmund rarely heard.

It had been worth slitting the throat of the white rabbit, after all.

Master Zeale leapt up, throwing back his blanket. He pranced around the room clad only in his hose, boasting, 'We're actually awake on a Moonsleep day! All the nobles will come to me begging for my potion. I'll be rich beyond the dreams of avarice.'

Edmund shared his excitement. Every male above the age of three had not woken during Moonsleep for the last two hundred years. They all slept in their beds for the three days and nights of the full moon.

'Now, get up and get dressed,' Master Zeale ordered.

Edmund obediently got up and started putting his hose on.

'Not those clothes,' Master Zeale said, and gave Edmund a clout around the head.

He staggered a little from the blow and rubbed his ear before asking, 'Which clothes then?'

'Are you an idiot? I told you, we're going to put on women's clothes so we can spy on the women without them recognising us.'

Edmund's heart sank. So, Master Zeale still wanted to go ahead with his silly idea of spying on the women.

'Couldn't we stay here for the rest of Moonsleep?' he asked. They knew the potion worked. What more did they need?

His master clouted him again. 'Stupid boy! The women'll get suspicious if they see smoke from this house during Moonsleep. They know no women live here.'

Edmund put on the chemise, the brown kirtle and surcoat Master Zeale had purchased for him on his last trip away from home. Then he pulled the wimple over his head to disguise his chin length hair. He'd hoped his master had changed his mind about going out. Master Zeale, dressed in an ankle-length kirtle, surcoat and wimple, looked like a skinny woman with a full moustache and beard. That was strange. Normally, Master Zeale had little facial hair.

'Master, you need to shave,' he told him.

Master Zeale stroked his beard. 'Indeed, I do. Let's breakfast, I'll shave and we'll go outside.'

Edmund followed his master out of the house. To his relief, there were no women in their narrow street made dark by the overhanging gables. His gaze was on the muck and rubbish strewn about the mud street, which is why he bumped into a woman. Edmund started.

'Beg pardon,' he gabbled. He looked up.

Mistress Brand, a tall middle-aged woman, smiled at them.

'I haven't seen you before.'

Edmund tried to speak but nothing came out. His tongue seemed to have swollen, filling his mouth. Master Zeale wasn't so afflicted.

'I'm Mistress Steel, and this is my daughter Mary, from Dartford. We've come to visit our kinsman Master Zeale,' said Zeale in a falsetto that had Edmund stifle a giggle.

'Master Zeale? The apothecary?'

'Yes,' squeaked Master Zeale.

Mistress Brand's smile dimmed. 'Then I hope you have a pleasant stay.' She moved past, then stopped. 'Do you know where the Ceremony will be held?'

'No,' Master Zeale squeaked.

'It's at the archery fields. Anyone can tell you where they are.' She walked off without giving them time to thank her. Not that Master Zeale would have done her the courtesy.

'Nosy busybody,' Master Zeale muttered. 'Thinks she's such a good apothecary.'

And so did most of the townsfolk, Edmund thought, to judge from the few customers that came to their shop.

'Did you hear that, Edmund?' He quivered with excitement. 'A ceremony? I knew they were up to no good during Moonsleep. Did she say when it was going to be held?'

'No, master.' Edmund shook his head.

Master Zeale cuffed him. 'What did I tell you? Don't call me master. We need to find out when the Ceremony is going to take place.'

They strolled around the town. Curiosity got the better of Edmund and he gazed about. Strange to see only women about. Master Zeale was always ranting about what the women got up to during Moonsleep. They seemed to be doing the usual things in Edmund's opinion: working, shopping, haggling, gossiping. They hovered near women queuing at a butcher's and heard one woman say, 'Goodbye. I'll see you after moonrise at the Ceremony.'

They returned to the apothecary's shop. Master Zeale was eager to see if his books had any mention of this ceremony. He had an extensive collection of documents gathered through the years. Every time he came back from one of his trips, he had another one. He spent most of his money on books. That and wine.

He pored over a few volumes, while Edmund put the sacrificial rabbit to simmer in a pot on the fire.

'It's no use,' Master Zeale lamented later at supper. 'Several commentaries speculate that women are to blame for the Curse, but none of them mention a ceremony.

And I couldn't find a spell to wake the other men without using the potion.'

'You could make a big batch of the potion next month to keep more men awake.' Edmund tensed, expecting a blow or a curse.

'Not a bad idea,' Master Zeale conceded as he slurped the rest of his bowlful. 'I'll write an account of the Ceremony and you can be my witness. Is there any more stew?'

Edmund ladled out another bowlful. Master Zeale consumed this too. 'Is there any more?' he asked to Edmund's surprise. Greediness was not one of his master's many faults.

'No, master,' he lied, hoping to save some for another supper.

Master Zeale looked for himself and then gave Edmund a resounding thwack for lying to him. He finished it, much to Edmund's annoyance. Master Zeale's beard had grown back again. And had his hands always been that hairy?

'We'll go early to the archery fields. Get ourselves a good position.'

'You need to shave again first, master.'

'That's strange. Perhaps it's a side effect of the potion. It might have more than one use.' He smiled, probably thinking of the profit to be made.

Master Zeale shaved with the aid of the bronze disk they used as a mirror. He cursed at Edmund to hold the disk straight. Edmund for once was glad he had no facial hair yet.

After supper, a knock on the front door made them jump. They stared at each other.

'Answer the door and see who it is,' Master Zeale ordered Edmund.

Edmund pulled the door with more force than he had intended. It flew open and banged against him, hiding him from view.

'Good night. I'm Mistress Sarah Tyndale. My boy Edmund is an apprentice here. I heard Master Zeale had kinsfolk visiting, and I wanted to meet you. May I come in?'

'Come in,' called Master Zeale in his falsetto voice.

Edmund's mother stepped through the doorway. She was not alone. Two burly Sheriff's Women marched behind her as she walked into the shop.

'Master Zeale, I am Mistress Cavendish of the Sheriff's Women. We want you to come with us to answer some questions,' the tall Sheriff's Woman said. Her grizzled grey hair showed she was the oldest of the three.

For a long moment, there was silence. Then Master Zeale roared and sprang forward. He hit the women so hard, they flew across the room and sprawled against the counters. Bottles rained down on them. Master Zeale ran out of the shop.

'After him,' shouted Mistress Cavendish, standing up.

The two youngest Sheriff's Women picked themselves up and ran out.

Edmund rushed to his mother. She lay still in a huddled heap, and for a horrible moment, he feared she was dead.

Then she opened her blue eyes and looked up into his face.

'Edmund?'

Edmund nodded and helped her to her feet.

Mistress Cavendish strode over to him and grabbed him by the arm. 'Where is he going?' she demanded.

'I think he's going to the Ceremony,' Edmund told her.

Mistress Cavendish turned to his mother. 'Sarah, you and the boy run to the archery fields and warn the abbess. I'll return to the Armoury, get more officers and some spears, and join you there. Are there any weapons here?' She left the shop.

Edmund pulled two stout cudgels from behind the counter. He handed one to his mother.

'Bring the other one,' his mother ordered. 'You might need it.'

He stepped out into the street. Edmund stopped short. The moon hung in the night sky, a beautiful white luminous globe with a soft radiance around it. He'd never seen a full moon before. His mother's description, when he'd asked her, had not prepared him for its beauty.

His mother cannoned into him.

'What are you doing?'

'The moon,' Edmund breathed, 'it's so beautiful.'

His mother gave him a push. 'You can gawk at the moon later. Come on!'

They both ran through the dark streets, towards the main gate and the archery fields that lay beyond. Women walking in twos and threes in the same direction, called out, but his mother wasted no time answering them and sped on.

At last, they were outside the town. The fields were dark, although the radiant moonlight helped. Edmund stumbled over the turf but followed the flickering lights and white figures up ahead in a circle.

As they grew closer, the lights became candles held by the nuns from the nearby abbey. The Daughters of Our Lady of the Moon were wearing white instead of their usual black habits. There was a rough wooden table in the middle of the circle. The small, slim abbess and Mistress Brand stood in front of it.

His mother pushed through the women already gathered there to approach the abbess.

'I've come to warn you, Abbess Berengaria,' she gasped. 'There's a man loose. Mistress Cavendish has gone for help, but we all need to get away from here!'

The abbess regarded her for a moment and then shook her head. 'The Ceremony must take place so that men do not wake up during Moonsleep. Forewarned is forearmed. We will start the Ceremony as soon as Mistress Cavendish and her women arrive.'

While they waited for the Sheriff's Women, more women joined the crowd. Edmund wondered if all the townswomen had come out tonight. The crowd murmured. At last, Mistress Cavendish and the extra women arrived, carrying spears and cudgels. They took up places in the crowd.

Then the abbess spoke. 'Welcome daughters, to our ceremony of remembrance and renewal. Every month, we perform this ritual so that the blessing of Moonsleep may continue. Let us always revere the memory of Queen Matilda and the holy women who created this miracle for us.'

The crowd murmured amen. Why did the abbess call it a blessing? Everyone knew that Moonsleep was a curse.

'This month, Mistress Juliana Brand has been chosen to make the offering.'

Abbess Berengaria stepped back. A nun came forward from the circle carrying a bowl and a knife. She bowed and offered the knife to Mistress Brand, who made a small incision on her left thumb and held it over the bowl. A few drops of blood dripped out.

'Let this blood symbolise the blood of all women and that of Mary, Holy Mother of God. Let the ritual begin.'

The nun rejoined her fellow nuns still carrying the bowl, and they all walked in a circle. The surrounding women began to chant, as did the nuns.

'Let the men sleep as the full moon shines…'

Screams rang out. An enormous wolf darted through the women. Only the scraps of garment clinging to its dark fur identified it as Master Zeale. The wolf howled and bounded towards the circle. Women around Edmund screamed. It attacked a nun and clawed at her before moving on. As it ran towards the abbess, she shouted, 'Fulgur percutiens!' and a bolt of bright green light hit it. The wolf staggered back and fell down, but within seconds it was back on its feet. It charged towards Abbess Berengaria and swiped at her with its claws. A dark stain bloomed on the white sleeve of her habit. Mistress Brand pointed at the wolf and shouted, 'Fulgur percutiens!' Another bolt struck it. Mistress Cavendish threw a spear that hit the wolf in its right foreleg. The wolf staggered and fell.

Two of the Sheriff's Women ran up to the prone wolf and swung their cudgels.

'Come on,' his mother said and ran to help them. Edmund did the same. He couldn't let the women fight the wolf on their own. His mother swung the cudgel and hit the wolf on the back. Together, they belaboured the wolf. The wolf turned, and he smashed the cudgel across its jaw. It yelped in protest. The wolf tried to rise, and they all smashed their cudgels down on it. Finally, it lay on the ground, quivering.

'Step aside,' ordered the voice of the abbess that brooked no disobedience.

They stepped aside. The abbess and Mistress Brand stepped up to the body of the wolf.

'Donec excitare, vos manet conscientiam, in nomine domina lunae,' they chanted in unison.

Mistress Brand nodded. 'That should hold him for a while.'

Edmund sagged. He shivered. Master Zeale had become a monster. His mother dropped her cudgel and put her arms around him.

'Everything's all right now,' she told him. 'The Reverend Mother will take care of everything.'

Abbess Matilda said, 'Take the monster to the abbey hospital.' She looked at Edmund. 'And bring the boy too.'

Edmund had thought he would be humiliated and embarrassed if they caught him in women's clothing, but now he was just scared.

'He's my son,' his mother said.

'Then you had better come too. Wait for us at the abbey while we complete the Ceremony.'

At the abbey, they ushered Edmund and Sarah to the parlour. It was silent. Edmund sat down on a wooden settle. His hands trembled, and he was cold. His mother sat next to him and put her arms around him. The warmth of her body, so close, comforted him.

'What happened, Edmund?' she asked.

He poured out the entire story to her.

A short while later, Mistress Brand came in with two pewter mugs.

'Here, drink this,' she said, handing one to Edmund.

Steam curled up from the mug. Edmund took the mug and sipped. Mistress Brand handed a mug to Sarah, and she drank.

'Drink up,' Mistress Brand urged. 'It'll do you good.'

The hot drink tasted of spices and warmed up Edmund. His eyelids fluttered. He tried to force them open, but it was a losing battle. He soon fell asleep.

A hand on his shoulder shook him. It was a nun, now dressed in a black habit.

'The Reverend Mother wants you.'

The parlour was lit with early morning light. Edmund and his mother followed her to the abbess' parlour. Abbess Berengaria sat behind a large desk. Mistress Brand, Mistress Cavendish, and an elderly nun stood nearby.

Abbess Berengaria now wore a clean white habit. She surveyed him; a scrutiny that made him writhe. 'So, this is the wolf's accomplice, dressed as a girl.'

Edmund's face burned with shame.

'He's Master Zeale's apprentice. He made Edmund dress up and spy on us,' Sarah said. 'He's not to blame.'

'I'll be the judge of that. Tell me, boy, how you two came to be awake.'

Edmund stumbled over his explanation of the spell and the potion to the circle of stern faces.

'Hmm.' The abbess turned to the elderly nun. 'Sister Beatrice, how fares Sister Elizabeth?'

'She's badly injured. We've done the best we could. It's in God's hands now.'

'And the wolf?'

'The spell you cast at the Ceremony will keep him sleeping until Moonsleep is over.'

'So, the question is – do we kill him?'

Edmund listened in horror.

'God knows we have cause,' said Mistress Cavendish. 'But it could provoke too much curiosity amongst the men about his death during Moonsleep. Best keep him alive, say I.'

The abbess inclined her head. 'And if we keep him alive?'

'We could cast the forgetting spell on him,' Sister Beatrice suggested.

Abbess Matilda smiled. 'Good. Will it work?'

'Oh yes, he will never remember who he was or what he did before.'

Edmund stared at the women in amazement. Were they all witches?

'Now for the boy. We should cast the forgetfulness spell on him too. Keep him at the abbey and lock him up every Moonsleep,' the abbess said.

Edmund gasped with horror. He didn't want to lose his memory or be imprisoned at the abbey.

'But he didn't turn into one!' cried his mother. Her hand tightened on his shoulder.

'He might turn into one next Moonsleep or in the future. Perhaps he's too young yet. And he could tell the men about this.'

'But we have no proof he will turn into a werewolf,' Mistress Brand said. 'To wipe all his memories without that, surely it would be a sin?'

There was a silence.

'Give me an alternative,' the abbess said.

'Could we not ask him to swear an oath that he will not tell the men about the Ceremony?' asked Mistress Brand. She looked compassionately at Edmund. 'On pain of his immortal soul?'

'I'll do that,' Edmund said eagerly.

'We could do that,' agreed Abbess Berengaria, not even glancing at Edmund. 'But can we be sure he won't be tempted to reveal the secret? Perhaps while in his cups. Would we be right to inflict him with such a burden?'

'I wouldn't!' said Edmund.

'Who would believe him?' Sarah asked. 'The testimony of one boy.'

Abbess Berengaria smiled. 'The men tell us, 'One man is worth twenty women'. Master Zeale's 'unfortunate accident' might make them willing to listen to him.' The abbess turned to Mistress Cavendish. 'Margaret, would Sheriff Wardham believe him?'

Mistress Cavendish considered this, her head tilted to one side. 'He might,' she said finally. 'He dislikes the Sheriff's Women… unlike his father, the old sheriff, God rest his soul.'

'Can we take this risk? For the sake not only of ourselves but of our sisters and daughters and future generations? If the men ever found out we deliberately created Moonsleep, we know what they would do.'

'What would they do?' asked Edmund.

'They would take your mother, rack her, torture her and then if she were lucky, hang her. Otherwise burn her at the stake. They would do that to all of us.' The abbess glanced around the room. The women's faces were sombre. 'You wouldn't want that to happen to your mother, would you, Edmund?'

He shook his head. How he wished that Master Zeale hadn't cast the spell, and he was fast asleep, dreaming about the moon.

'We could lock him up at the abbey every month until

we know whether he turns into a werewolf,' Sister Beatrice said.

'And once we were sure he wasn't a werewolf, he could stay home,' his mother said.

'If he proves to be a werewolf, he must always come to the abbey,' Abbess Berengaria said.

She nodded. 'I agree.'

'And if you promise to remain quiet about this, Edmund, I'll promise to take him as my apprentice, Sarah. Let him learn how to be a proper apothecary,' said Mistress Brand.

Abbess Berengaria looked at Edmund. 'Come here.'

The boy stood in front of her. She took off her moon cross and held it out to him. 'Kiss the cross and swear by God, Jesus, the Holy Spirit, and Mary, Mother of God that you will never reveal this secret, on pain of torments in this life and the next.'

Edmund repeated her words. She nodded. He stepped back next to his mother. Sagging with relief, he heard little of their next discussion. They decided Master Zeale should be taken to his shop. Sarah would come by in the morning to help Edmund with the discovery.

Edmund awoke. Sunlight streamed into the room through the narrow windows. Moonsleep was over for another month. Normal life could resume again. Perhaps the events of last night hadn't happened, and it was just a dream. The other pallet was empty. Master Zeale might be downstairs. He got up, dressed, and went to investigate.

Master Zeale lay at the bottom of the stairs, motionless.

Edmund thundered down them. Purple bruises covered his master's face, and his nose was bent out of shape. His right leg was bandaged. Edmund bent down to check that he was breathing, that the women hadn't killed him after all. Breath fluttered his ear.

A knock came at the door downstairs. Edmund ran down to open it. His mother stood there, a welcome sight, holding two freshly baked loaves. The aroma made Edmund's mouth water.

'Come in, Mother.'

She stepped inside and looked at the body of his master.

'I'd best put these loaves in the kitchen, and we can get started. Run to the abbey and ask one of the nuns from the infirmary to come. Tell them it's urgent.'

Edmund came back with the Infirmarer herself, Sister Beatrice. The elderly nun checked his master over and straightened up.

'He's no worse than last night. Run back to the abbey – Edmund, is it? – and tell Sister Agnes, to sort out a cart to bring him there.'

Edmund did as he was told. He was doing a lot of running today on an empty stomach. He was a little ashamed he was thinking of that rather than his injured master.

They took away the sleeping Master Zeale.

'Have some breakfast, Edmund,' his mother said. 'You can't do anything for him now but there's no sense you starving.'

Edmund sat himself down by the kitchen table and

tore into a loaf. After a few minutes – Moonsleep always made him extra hungry – asked, 'What happens now?'

'Master Zeale will remain at the abbey. He'll be locked up every Moonsleep, but he'll be well cared for.'

Edmund knew he should feel sorry for him losing all his memories and knowledge, but Zeale had never been a good master and now he was a dangerous monster. He felt sorrier for himself.

'I must go to the abbey every Moonsleep,' he groused.

'Only until we're sure you're not a werewolf. Better than losing your memory,' his mother reminded him. 'And you'll become Mistress Brand's apprentice. You'll become an apothecary.'

Edmund wondered if he would ever see another full moon.

THE TEMPTATION OF
CHARLOTTE BRONTE

The parsonage, despite possessing twelve rooms, was not large enough to contain her frustration and bitter disappointment. Charlotte flung herself out to tramp on the moors. But the vast tranquillity and harsh beauty did not work its usual magic of soothing her nerves and comforting her fears.

'Two copies sold of our volume of poetry! Only two copies!' she screeched at the uncaring sky. 'I would sell my soul to the Devil,' she shouted at the bracken and the sheep, 'for a novel that would sell thousands of copies.'

She closed her eyes, imagining publishers baying for the right to publish her work, herself lionised in London literary circles, and meeting her hero, William Thackeray.

The cry of a curlew opened her eyes. There was a gentleman, not two feet away from her, clad in a greatcoat and muffler. Where had he come from? Charlotte's cheeks burned with shame that he had heard her outburst. He took off his glossy black top hat.

'Do I have the honour of addressing the famous author, Miss Charlotte Bronte?'

'You mock me, sir,' Charlotte snapped and turned to go.

'Or should I say – the soon to be famous Miss Charlotte

Bronte – if you accept my offer? Allow me to introduce myself. I am called the Prince of Darkness or Lucifer, Satan, Beelzebub, you may take your pick of the names, I answer to them all.'

Charlotte quickened her step. She was alone on the moors with a madman.

'If you sell your soul to me, you will have everything you desire,' he said behind her.

Charlotte turned round and shouted at him, 'Leave me alone!'

'I see I need to convince you of my credentials. Perhaps, we could continue this conversation in a more congenial location. I must confess, I am used to a warmer climate.'

Charlotte felt the wind howl around her, whipping her skirt and cloak about her.

Then she was back home, in the empty parlour. Emily must be in the kitchen and Anne probably at her prayers. Her heart stopped for a long moment and then beat very rapidly. She gaped at the gentleman who now lounged in an armchair, his outer garments gone. She saw, astonished, his dark, saturnine features bore a strong resemblance to the hero of her youthful stories, the Duke of Zamorna. There was a cup and saucer steaming on the table. He gestured towards it.

'I thought a restorative cup of tea for you?'

She sank down onto a hard chair.

'Now to business. You said aloud you would sell your soul for writing a great work of literature that sold thousands of copies?'

'I didn't mean it.'

'You could not have summoned me if you hadn't meant it.'

'Can you really do that?' she asked.

'But, of course,' the Devil assured her. 'One soul in exchange for a masterpiece and a lifetime of wealth and fame. How many women have written a great work of literature?'

Charlotte hesitated. 'I'm not sure.'

'Come now, to be recognised and feted as a great writer?' He gazed at her, head on one side. 'Wait! I have had an idea,' he continued. 'I have just had an interesting notion, which is very welcome. You would pity me if you had any idea of the vast ocean of ennui that I am engulfed in.'

Charlotte thought that she would never feel sorry for the Devil, no matter the circumstances.

'Let me elaborate. What if you sold me your soul, in exchange for writing a classic *and* making your life a happier and more pleasant one?'

'I don't understand.;

'Allow me to demonstrate.'

The Devil twirled his hand and the parlour disappeared.

Charlotte was standing in a cold and barely furnished bedroom. There was a narrow bed with two young girls huddled together for warmth under a thin coverlet.

'You know where this is, don't you, Charlotte?'

Charlotte started. 'It's Cowan Bridge,' she said

'Indeed, it is, and the year is 1825.'

'The year Maria died,' she said with a sob.

'I'm afraid it is. You wake up in the morning with your arms around Maria, only to find that your beloved elder sister has died in the night.'

Charlotte nodded. Tears welled up in her eyes.

'This would be the bargain. Maria does not die but lives to a ripe old age. Wouldn't you like that?'

'It's not possible,' Charlotte whispered.

'Of course, it's possible. I'm the Devil. Aren't you tempted?'

Charlotte could not speak. A tear trailed down one cheek.

'Or perhaps there is another event in your life that might tempt you more.'

The Devil waved his hand again and the scene vanished to be replaced by another parlour where a middle-aged man with long black side-whiskers sat. He was reading a letter, frowning. When he had finished, he crumpled it up and threw it onto the fire, blazing blue and red-gold in the grate.

'You remember this, don't you, Charlotte?' the Devil taunted her. 'It's the school in Brussels where you met Constantin Héger and fell deeply in love with him. But he did not return your affection, or your letters and you were broken-hearted for years afterwards.'

The tears in Charlotte's eyes overflowed and ran down her cheeks.

'You could come here, and Constantin would fall in love with you.'

'He's married,' Charlotte said.

The Devil dismissed this with a 'Pah! Easily solved. Madame Héger could suffer a brief devastating illness and die or perhaps a fatal accident. You could choose, you never liked her much, did you?'

'Then I would have the death of a Christian soul on my conscience,' Charlotte cried.

'The death of a woman you don't like against married to the love of your life. Is that so great a price to pay?'

'I cannot choose my happiness at the expense of another's life. I would prefer to have Maria alive.'

'Oh, dear me, I forgot to tell you this,' the Devil said. 'I should have explained. Someone else must die if someone lives who should have died.'

'Who?'

'Emily.'

'Emily?' Charlotte asked. Her skin grew cold and clammy as she thought of life without her sister Emily.

'I know what you are thinking. Why not Bramwell?'

'I was not thinking that! Bramwell does his best,' Charlotte defended her only brother.

'He certainly does his best to be a reprobate and disgrace to his family,' the Devil mused. 'However, let us keep to the point. Emily must die if Maria lives. Of course, it would mean the loss of 'Wuthering Heights' but how could that compare to the joy of having your sister Maria with you all your life? And if she is as clever and talented as the rest of your family, she may well write a classic herself.'

'I would then have Emily's death on my conscience,' Charlotte pointed out through clenched teeth.

'But you would have your darling Maria *and* a masterpiece. There is always a price to pay. Are you not tempted by either your sister or your beloved? I'll tell you what. I will leave you for one hour to ponder these choices and then I will return to make the exchange.'

He bowed to her. He vanished and the parlour reappeared.

Charlotte rested her head on her arms on the parlour table. How was she to choose? Maria or Emily? Maria or Constantin? Why was the Devil tormenting her like this? Why had he added another inducement to the deal? The more she thought about it, the more she was convinced that there must be something suspicious about the offer. Also, he had mentioned a work by Emily. Was Emily destined to be one of the greats of literature? How could Charlotte deny her that? She choked a little as she thought about it. Her dearest wish was to be a famous author.

The Devil reappeared an hour later. 'Punctuality is the politeness of kings,' he said. 'And devils.' He smirked.

Charlotte raised her head from her arms.

'Have you made up your mind? Which did you choose? Your sister or your beloved? I admit, I am quite agog.'

Charlotte stood up and pushed back the chair. 'I have made up my mind,' she told him.

'Which one is it?'

'I have decided not to take up your offer.'

The Devil frowned and red embers glowed in his dark eyes. 'You do not want to sell your soul?'

'No, I have changed my mind.'

'Think of what you would be losing,' the Devil pleaded.

'I have. I think you have only offered me Maria or Constantin to make me choose the bargain. There is something you are not telling me, something to your advantage. I would be a fool to sign away my soul without all the facts. Also, I have come to realise that if I cannot write a great work of literature by my own efforts then I do not deserve to reap the rewards. I thank you for that.'

The Devil glared at her. 'The day will come when you find it impossible to refuse my offer, madam!'

He stamped his foot and disappeared in a great cloud of black smoke. The acrid smell of brimstone hung in the air. The smoke slowly evaporated.

Charlotte took a great breath. 'I had best start writing my masterpiece and prove I do not need the Devil's help,' she said to the silent parlour.

AFTERWORD

I'd love to know what you think of my stories. Please leave a review on Amazon or Goodreads. Your feedback is like gold dust for indie authors.

If you notice any typos, as can happen with the best intentions and proof reading, please let me know at liz@liztuckwell.co.uk.

For a free copy of *The Snowman Nightmare* and updates on my writing and other interesting titbits, please sign up for my mailing list at:

landing.mailerlite.com/webforms/landing/s1n7r2

ABOUT THE AUTHOR

Liz Tuckwell writes quirky dark fantasy, science fiction and horror stories.

She lives in North West London and currently shares her house with a husband and too many books. She has an identical twin sister. Liz enjoys reading and writing all types of science fiction, fantasy and horror, and fitting in as many holidays as she can into a year when there isn't a pandemic. She's a member of the Clockhouse London Writers group and the British Fantasy Society.

You can find out more about Liz at:

www.liztuckwell.co.uk.

facebook.com/LizTuckwell1Author

twitter.com/@liztuckwell1

instagram.com/liztuckwell01

ALSO BY LIZ TUCKWELL

Fantastic Flash Fiction

Quirky Christmas Stories

The Raven King

Printed in Great Britain
by Amazon

82914967R00120